HOT
HIGHLANDERS
AND WILD WARRIORS

EROTIC ROMANCE FOR WOMEN

EDITED BY DELILAH DEVLIN

FOREWORD BY TERRY SPEAR

**TEMPTED
ROMANCE**

Published in the United States by Tempted Romance, an imprint
of Cleis Press, Inc., 2246 Sixth Street, Berkeley, California 94710.

Printed in the United States.
Cover design: Scott Idleman/Blink
Cover photograph: Hot Damn Stock
Text design: Frank Wiedemann

First Edition.
10 9 8 7 6 5 4 3 2 1

Trade paper ISBN: 978-1-940550-02-2
E-book ISBN: 978-1-940550-07-7

Contents

Foreword

Terry Spear

My ancestors were Highlanders of old, and so I love to envision those hot hunks—and they were tall even way back then—in their kilts and tunics, wielding claymore swords, wearing *sgian dubhs* in their boots, managing a hard life and surviving. Their women were just as adventurous, just as hardy, and would fight alongside their men, bear their children, love them, and who wouldn't? One of my ancestors was the Duke of Argyll's daughter and she ran off with a commoner because she loved the Highlander so and he loved the Highland lady just as much in return. When a woman gives up everything to be with the Highlander she loves, that is the most endearing and romantic sacrifice anyone can make.

I've been to Scotland, visited seven castles, and felt at home in the ruins of one sitting high above the North Sea. I've been shielded from the cold wind by the castle walls, knelt beside the well in the center of the grassy bailey, explored the rooms where the laird and lady once slept and imagined being there with my own Highland laird, kilted and rugged, sexy smile and all.

But it's not only the Highlanders who deserve praise as men of an ancient period who were worth doting on. Though they often have a bad rap, the Vikings—or men of the North as they themselves were really known—were family oriented, wonderful explorers, traders, settlers, farmers, mighty warriors and loyal to kin like the Highlanders were. What could be hotter than curling up with a Viking, wrapped in furs, ready for him to start your own fire burning? And the best? Women were treated as equals in the Viking household. A wife held the keys, and in their marriage, if a husband didn't live up to her expectations or insulted her family or her, he was out of there. Just a declaration of divorce in front of witnesses at their front door and bed, and the deed was done. Bathing was important to them as well, and they had heated bathhouses; in the summer, they swam in the lakes and the rivers. Washing their faces and hands, and washing and combing out their hair were normal everyday activities. When a woman washed her man's hair, it was intimate indeed. It was said that the men were so clean, they stole ladies away from the English, who didn't bathe nearly as often!

Or what about the chain mail-clad knight, his tunic covered in the family emblem, fighting to protect hearth and home? And now he's returned to you, and what's a good lady to do? Help him out of all that mail, then bathe him in a wooden tub, the fire burning at the hearth, the curtained bed ready for the two of you? It's reported that one of my ancestors was Lady Godiva, and so I am just as enamored with the ways of the ladies and knights of the English courts, of the courtly gestures and fascinating goings-on of the period. At one point, men's fashion changed so that the tunic became shorter and shorter and shorter. But they didn't have pants like we do today. So they had to cover up their endowments. That meant wearing a codpiece.

Isn't history and the ancient man fascinating? It was said that one royal personage wore such a large codpiece, the ladies and gentlemen could see it before he entered the room. But before this, the men's armored shoes were designed with pointier and pointier toes and about that time, they would wiggle them suggestively at the women, whereupon they would giggle in delight, until the church condemned such behavior. Knights will be knights, you know. So truly, what's not to love in those fighting, protective, loyal and sexy men of old?

Terry Spear
Author of The Highlanders series

INTRODUCTION

I'm a romance writer, but before that, I was a reader of romance novels and my favorites were historical stories set in medieval times. Genres rise and fall in popularity, but medieval romances, whether about knights in shining armor or Highlanders in their tartans, are always there. So I was thrilled to have the chance to put together a collection of stories set in long-ago times in faraway places.

I asked authors to let their fantasies run wild to an era where men wearing heavy armor or thick tartans sent a spirited young maiden's (or salty widow's) heart fluttering. What I received were stories set in Scotland and England, as well as Iceland, Japan, Rome, France and Armenia, with knights, Highlanders, Vikings, Mongols and even a Samurai. There's certainly a warrior among these tales to suit every taste, and sexy battles of dominance and submission hot enough to make even the most modern women yearn to be taken by one of these rough, fierce men.

Delilah Devlin

Pleasure in Surrender

Delilah Devlin

Kent, England, 1067 AD

The first missive arrived without fanfare, passed through the iron bars of the barbican by a lone messenger dressed entirely in black.

Sir Geade read the note, lifted a graying brow and then passed the small scroll to Lady Edwina, who held it beneath the oak table to read it. Not that everyone wasn't aware of the queer fact that she could read.

Prepare for a wedding or a siege.

With all gazes resting on her, Edwina schooled her expression into a neutral mask. "Should I thank him for the warning, Geade?"

Sir Geade snorted. "He gives us time to retreat to the keep, stock the larders and call our neighbors for assistance. Perhaps we should."

"What sort of warrior would give away his plan?" she murmured, not the least bit alarmed. *Not yet.*

"Either a fool or one who's supremely confident."

She traced the bold scrawl scratched across the parchment with her fingertip, knowing instinctively the bold knight had written the message himself. No proud scribe would pen a note so spare.

Grimvarr had been written across the bottom—as if she should already know his name and the two syllables should strike fear. "An odd name for a Norman knight." As she swept from the hall, she would never have admitted that the word *wedding* had caused her more alarm than *siege*.

In response to the warning, Edwina ordered the stores replenished and the flocks of sheep brought closer to the keep, but otherwise went about her business without worry.

Who was this baseborn knight with designs on her demesne? Her overlord had assured her the choice of a husband from among the eligible men in the region—once her grief was passed. That Edwina had every intention of nursing her grief for as many years as she could was a secret she kept to herself.

But by the time the second missive arrived, she'd learned a thing or two about the mysterious Grimvarr. Lord Alred's steward had been a font of gossip concerning the knight who'd earned the Duke of Normandy's trust by barreling into the royal pretender to save him from an assassin's arrow. That act had earned him the gift of her demesne. A fact she found humiliating to learn in such a manner, but since her overlord had yet to apprise her directly of the news, she preferred to assume it was only rumor. How could the pretender give a gently bred woman to a barbarian?

Grimvarr was a Viking—or at least half the demon race, his father having abducted a Norman maiden and returned her promptly to her father when she'd spoiled his enjoyment by getting with child. And although he'd been raised by a Norman peer, Grimvarr chose to dress in the fur and skins of his barbarian father.

No doubt Alred's man had embellished the tale to cause Edwina worry. His master would love to see her squirm after she'd refused his latest suggested mate, claiming she'd marry the pig keeper before she'd wed a man who'd already sent two wives to the grave in childbirth.

While she kept her chin high and her comments derisive of her new "suitor" whenever he was mentioned in company, she'd suffered nightmares during the nights before the second note arrived.

This message was longer.

I bring twenty-five knights, a hundred bowmen, swords and shields to arm every man, and one siege machine. Yield to me or face consequences.

Geade grunted, but worry creased his rugged brow.

"'Tis a love letter," she muttered, determined to keep the bastard knight's looming menace from raising alarm among her people. "He intends to impress me. No different than any of the other preening knights who've tried to woo me."

"Perhaps he simply gives you fair warning, milady." At her reproving glance, Sir Geade shrugged. "Our requests for reinforcements from Alred and Rathburn have gone unanswered."

"They simply need time—"

"They know he approaches. Perhaps they fear him."

"He bluffs!" she said with a dismissive wave of her hand. "What landless bastard commands such a force?"

He sighed. "Perhaps you are right. However, I would sleep easier if you remained inside the walls—at least for the coming weeks," he amended when she gave him a scowl.

It rankled that her freedoms were curtailed by an upstart. Still, it was worrisome no one had answered her calls for assistance. Was he truly so imposing?

Her answer came one morning when the mists melted away to reveal glints of the armor and weapons of the force that spread across the meadow below the castle's dirt moat. Guards had alerted Sir Geade, who'd awoken her before dawn to tell her they had visitors.

As she strode the length of the curtain wall peering down at the small army, she felt her first real frisson of unease. It seemed the knight hadn't been bluffing after all.

Another note was passed. She held out her hand for the message, broke the seal, and unrolled the parchment. After a quick glance, she ripped the message to bits, tossing it over the castle walls. She hoped *Lord Grim's* eyesight was good, because she didn't want her response to his demand that she open the gates missed.

Indeed, a horse burst from the line of mounted knights and rushed forward to a spot well beyond her archers' aim. There, the warrior reined in his horse and stared up at the curtain wall. The man astride the huge black warhorse fixed her with a glare she couldn't miss despite the distance, and she shivered. Was it him? Good Lord, he was large, freakishly so, with shoulders made to appear even more broad by the black bear sash he wore over his armor. His arms were bare except for a wide golden band surrounding one thick bicep. His thighs were like tree trunks as he straddled his great warhorse. There was little she could see about his face other than the strong jut of his chin and sinfully dark gaze hidden behind the nosepiece of his conical Viking helm. Long dark hair waved from beneath his helmet.

As she gazed down, an unexpected thrill pulsed through her. Completely unwanted. Irresistibly mystifying. Why, after all the suitors she'd ousted from her keep, did this one make her breath hitch? Edwina drew a deep breath and slowly shook her head. It was only the thrill of the challenge he presented. She lifted her chin and turned her back.

Geade groaned beside her. "You'd add insult to your refusal?"

"He bluffs," she said with a wave of her hand even though she felt the giant's wicked gaze burning on her back. "We have the advantage. My mother withstood my father for months. The walls are strong, our stores of foodstuffs and weapons replete—thanks to his warnings. We have only to outwait him."

Geade's gaze went to the meadow; his gray brows furrowed with doubt. "I don't think this knight will wage a gentleman's campaign to win your heart, milady."

Edwina rolled her eyes. Her mother's siege had been a woman's ploy to force a husband she wanted to accede to her demands. And she'd won. She didn't need the old grizzled knight who'd witnessed her mother's strategy to remind her this time was far different.

Still, a siege was a siege regardless of the motives of either side. "We will not open the gates to this barbarian. Our neighbors will learn of this outrage, and they will come to our rescue. That or Lord Alred will put a stop to the Viking's campaign. I have his promise of protection."

Geade's breath whistled between his pursed lips. "I think not, milady."

At the jerk of his chin, she turned to gaze beyond the line of the Viking's contingent. Alred's banners waved behind them.

"He supports his suit?" she said, feeling faint.

Geade snorted. "He's likely come to enjoy the battle. The tale of your lady mother's victory provided entertainment for years."

Edwina pressed her lips together, not liking the hint of humor dancing in Geade's eyes. "I'm not my mother, and I'm not withholding my hand to ensure that I keep my wealth separate from my husband's. I'll not take a husband I don't want."

"Are you sure this is the battle you wish to fight, milady?"

Geade was her best friend, but she'd ignored his imploring that she find a husband to rule with her. She'd been blessed the first time with Malcolm. A man who'd left the running of the castle, the overseeing of the harvests, the tallying of the tithes to her while he'd drunk himself to death.

His excesses had nearly beggared them, and yet she'd managed to hide the extent of their wealth, and had hidden away enough to see them through hard times after his untimely death. Enough to allow her to pay a widow's pension to Lord Alred to ensure her period of mourning was respected. The fact she'd just made her annual payment galled, seeing his forces aligned behind the Viking's.

Edwina didn't flinch from the sight. Men betrayed women all the time. With a final internal reminder that she was indeed her mother's daughter, she shook back her hair. "Send the bastard our response."

Geade's lips firmed. She knew he wanted to say more, but he also knew when to keep silent. His cheeks billowed around an exasperated breath, but he nodded, raised an arm and dropped it. The arm of the catapult parked in the middle of the bailey snapped upward, and the contents held in the scooped arm sailed high over the walls.

Her own men ducked, faces screwing into ferocious grimaces,

but once the contents cleared the wall, they all turned toward the army at the bottom of the hill.

Shouts rang up and down the line, and arms rose to shield eyes as they stared upward. Edwina smirked as the foul contents of the castle's jakes rained down on the Viking's men. "Let the game begin."

After a nerve-wracking day that she'd spent supervising meals and finding places inside the bailey and keep for everyone to sleep, she was exhausted. But the moment she'd doused her candle and lain down on her bed, her doubts crowded in.

She would never allow her people to suffer through a long siege. It being May, they were needed in their fields. No, she had perhaps a week before she'd have to concede. She eased open her fists and drew long breaths. Sleep was what she needed. Perhaps in the morning she would hit upon a scheme to delay the inevitable or plead her case to Alred. She rolled onto her side, tucked her hands beneath her face and stared into the dark corners of her room.

Geade wondered about her objection. So did she. Was it only willful pride, tweaked by the fact she had no choice in the matter? It wasn't as though she didn't want a man, *someday*, to share her burdens and her bed. Then she remembered the sight of Grimvarr, so large and fiercely masculine.

Alone, she admitted a moment's wild excitement. Malcolm had never made her yearn for his embrace. And yet this Viking had somehow crept into her bed. What would it be like to submit to a man like him? One strong enough to subdue her, one who caused more than a flutter of heat to curl inside her womb?

A draft brushed her face. She'd closed the door and latched the pigskin curtain over her narrow window. A scuff of a foot had her stiffening, but she heard no more above the pounding of her heart. She wasn't alone. "Who's there?" she whispered.

"I think you know," came a deep, rumbling drawl.

She drew a deep breath and came up slowly, scooting to the far side of her bed. Her knife was on her chatelaine's belt hanging from a peg beside the door. She was weaponless. "My people?"

"Your man Geade surrendered as soon as he realized the keep was overrun. No one was harmed."

"How?"

"Does it matter? I've taken this castle. The only question now is one I want answered: Why did you bar the gates?"

Edwina shivered at his graveled voice. "I was promised time to grieve before I accepted another husband."

"Alred suspected you would grieve until you were old. Did you really think he would defy the king's order for you?"

She lifted her chin although she knew the gesture couldn't be seen—not unless Vikings had eyes like cats. "I expected him to honor his promise. I paid for the privilege."

"About that—he returned the gold. To me." His footsteps drew nearer her bed. "But that doesn't answer the question. Why, Edwina?"

Her mouth grew dry at the rasping texture of his deep voice. She swallowed and set her back against the wall. "I wed once for political expediency. This time, I wanted a choice."

He remained silent for a long moment. "And yet you have turned away every suitor who approached you."

"None were worthy."

"You hold yourself in such high esteem?"

"I worried for my people. Warriors don't make the best farmers."

His footsteps scraped closer.

She pressed harder against cold stone.

"I will admit, I've little experience with farming. But I understood you were competent. That I could rely on you to teach me."

He said the words slowly, and she tried to read his intentions in the inflections of his voice. Could he be telling her the truth? Would he allow her to continue as steward of her land? "Are we…negotiating?"

After a long moment, he cleared his throat. "You wed young."

"I had no choice, but Malcolm was malleable and a drunk. We came to an arrangement that suited us both. I managed the estate. He drank and caroused, spending from a generous budget. We were both satisfied."

"You managed him and the estate."

"Yes."

After a pause, he said, "I'm not malleable. Nor will I be managed."

She heard the steel in his tone. She forced a derisive note into her own. "I was afraid of that. It's why I closed the gates and prepared for a siege."

He strode closer. His large shadow was inky black, ominous. "You do realize this is our wedding night? You are already my wife by the king's decree. Only consummation awaits."

Alarm rattled through her. "But there must be a wedding. The banns should be read."

"No, Edwina. Your resistance ends tonight."

But his large frame strode away. Whispers sounded from the doorway. Moments later, light flooded the room. Servants carrying candles and chests entered, storing away his belongings—all the while averting their gazes from her.

And all she could do was stare at his towering frame, dressed in a boiled leather hauberk, chauses and soft leather boots. Dressed as lightly as he was, without armor, she guessed he and his men had scaled the walls.

And another realization scattered her thoughts. Grimvarr was a very handsome man with a square chin, a narrow strip of beard surrounding his mouth and chin, bladed cheeks and dark, hooded eyes. Combined with his large rugged frame, his appearance was imposing in its masculine perfection, and becoming even more imposing as he stripped.

When he was nude, she fought the temptation to drop her gaze to his groin. Something she found nearly impossible to do because the enormity of his cock struck her nonetheless at the periphery of her gaze.

"There is no reason to fear me, Edwina."

She swallowed hard. "You are here against my wishes."

Two red spots darkened his cheekbones.

Her insides quivered, but not from fear that she'd angered him. She couldn't drag her gaze from his body.

He approached the bed and sat on the edge of the mattress. So close, she was tempted to reach out to discover if his body was as hard as it appeared. She was his wife. She did have the right, and yet, she squared her shoulders in resistance.

"I will be gentle and quick. You need not fear me."

She let her gaze drop to his large cock. "How can you promise me gentleness?"

"If you will put your trust in me, I will show you." And then he held still. His large frame unmoving. Waiting for her answer. Something he didn't have to do. She already belonged to him. Every bit as much as her castle, her people and the large tract of her demesne. But it seemed he wanted her cooperation—her surrender, she amended. And shouldn't she try to appease him?

She was at his mercy, a thought that swirled endlessly in her mind. Years of Malcolm's debauchery had cooled her ardor, for a time, but lovers had entered her dreams. Was she foolish to believe there could be pleasure in surrender?

Glancing away from his dark eyes, she lowered the sheet she'd clutched against her chest. She pulled off her shift and tossed it to the floor, and then sat silently, afraid to glance his way, afraid to read into his expression because she knew she was slender, her breasts small, and didn't men prefer a more bountiful frame to slake their urges against?

A rasp against her tight nipple drew her gaze downward. His fingertip, so large and calloused, touched her with a surprising delicacy. Her nipple responded, blooming beneath his scrape, her areola dimpling as the tip ripened and protruded.

"Such a pretty pink," he murmured.

A blush heated her cheeks. "You don't have to praise me. I know that I am as thin as a pike."

"You think you lack womanly attributes?" he murmured.

"I am simply saying that you don't have to woo me with pretty phrases. I want this done. Over." *Liar.*

His jaw tightened, and he ripped back the sheet. "Very well. Prepare to receive me."

Her eyes widened.

His brow arched. "You wanted brevity."

"I did," she said feeling a little faint. But she did as he asked, scooting down the bed and stretching her legs. Now lying, she parted her thighs, crossed her arms over her chest and closed her eyes.

When he didn't move for the longest time, she peeked at him

from beneath her lashes. He was staring, a dark scowl twisting his face. Her belly tightened as she reminded herself there was much to fear in being alone with this man.

He cursed under his breath. "This will not be quick, Edwina."

"I am cooperating," she said, her voice shrill.

His sigh was deep. "This husband of yours, how did he manage the consummation?"

She shrugged. "He came on top of me, thrust a few times, and was done. Thankfully, his seed never took."

"Just the once?" he asked, arching a brow.

"Of course not, but he soon found others he enjoyed more, and who seemed to enjoy him."

"And you didn't mind that he shamed you?"

She cleared her throat. "I was relieved he didn't seek my bed. And he must not have found a fertile woman because he didn't leave his spawn littering the castle."

His eyes narrowed. "Are you really this harsh or does the act frighten you?"

"I'm not afraid." Not of him. Not of sex. She feared another disappointing experience. She raised her gaze to his, noted the hard light in his eyes and took a deep breath. "I am ready."

"You are not. By far, you are not. But then, it is my responsibility to school you, Edwina, to prove to you there is more to this act than something repulsive and demeaning." He raked a hand through his dark hair and blew out a harsh breath that billowed his cheeks. When he turned away and jerked open her chamber door, she stared.

Not until several minutes had passed did she understand that he'd left her. She almost smiled. She'd won. And then she remembered how he'd looked, large and brutish, but with dark eyes that glinted with a hint of wild promise, and her shoulders slumped. Had she finally met the man who could tempt her only to turn him away?

Edwina stubbornly went about her daily tasks the next morning, ignoring her added guests. There were so many people crowding the hall that she sent the villagers back to their homes and the shepherds to move the flocks outside the walls. The strangers among Alred's men, her husband's men, gave her surreptitious stares but kept silent, taking their cue from Grimvarr, who sat on the dais next to Alred, maps spread across the table while they drank and parlayed.

She tried to ignore her husband's steady stares, but every time his gaze rested on her, heat infused her body. She grew uncomfortable in her own skin and her clothing felt tight. Every time she claimed the nerve to meet his glance with a direct one of her own, she felt as though she was falling, leaning toward him, darkness closing around her sight, like she was looking through a tunnel where only he existed in the end.

Ridiculous! She wasn't falling. Wasn't afraid. Wasn't some half-witted slut lusting after a man. And yet, lust rose up so often throughout the day that she was nearly exhausted from fighting her inner turmoil. So much so, that after she'd seen to the dinner meal, she slipped away, retiring to her room. Hoping he'd never notice she'd shown weakness, but hoping too that he'd seek her out.

She wanted to matter to him. To be more than a means to wealth and privilege. Good Lord, she wanted *him*.

Behind her, the door creaked open. She glanced over her shoulder to find Grimvarr leaning his back against the door.

"Thank you for your efforts today. Alred had nothing but praise for your hospitality."

"As you already knew, I am a competent chatelaine," she said, lifting her chin, challenge thrown down, should he bother to accept.

"You do know that Alred will not quit this keep until we are truly wed."

She blinked, realizing he was giving her a strong reason to capitulate—one other than the fact desire swirled thick in the room, and so urgently she found it hard to unstick her tongue from the roof of her mouth to reply. But she did. "He and his men will eat and drink their way through the stores."

Grimvarr's lips twitched. And there in his dark eyes, she saw a glint of humor. Something that eased the stiffness of her back. There was a sly wit beneath his brutish appearance. Intelligence beyond his prowess on the battlefield. And a lambent heat in his dark eyes that spoke to her across the silence. He wasn't asking for surrender. Rather, he sought her cooperation to achieve a common goal. He was saving her pride. A concession as a sign of respect. Could she offer him no less?

Slowly, Edwina reached for the ties at her shoulders and pulled at the soft knots, beginning to disrobe. "We should save the best wines for the harvest celebration in the fall." There, she'd told him she no longer objected to this union.

His mouth stretched slowly, and he too began to strip. In minutes, they stood nude, gazes raking the other's frame until she took the initiative and slipped backward onto the mattress.

He followed, coming over her, bracing his weight on his arms, his glance sliding down her narrow frame, then up again, and centering on her mouth. "You have a generous mouth."

She sniffed, pretending more confidence than she felt. His weight pinned her to the bed. "It is large."

"I am large, and one day you will understand how perfectly we suit."

He said it with a crooked smile, but she was breathless, too excited to wonder what he meant, because he bent toward her and rubbed his mouth against hers. His kiss was softer than she'd expected, but demanding all the same, lips slanting and drawing on hers, waiting until she followed his circular motions, acceding to the kiss.

When his teeth bit her lower lip, she gasped and his tongue entered her, surprising her. His tongue slid along the meat of hers, lashing it, rimming her teeth.

They kissed with their eyes wide open—her eyes crossing from the nearness, his smoldering. Without thought, she tightened her lips and suctioned on his tongue.

A groan passed from his mouth into hers, and she gave it back, at last closing her eyes and simply feeling the way he patiently prodded and licked, awakening something inside her—a curl of heat, deep inside her womb.

He was large and brutal, this she knew from the stories she'd heard, but he was also terribly insistent—and he would make sure she enjoyed this, whether she wanted to or not.

And suddenly...*she wanted*. Desperately. Again, she remembered him breaking from the line astride his warhorse, his body frighteningly large, his dark hair fluttering from beneath his conical helm. She'd felt a shiver of unwanted attraction and tamped it down. He'd looked like a Norse god come to life, but she'd feared he'd be every bit as brutish. And yet, here he was, set on seducing her.

By the time he drew back, breaking the kiss, she was breathing heavily, her nipples hard points catching in the fur of his chest. She wanted to rub against him, chafe in the silky curls.

His hands framed her face; his thumbs caressed her bottom lip. "Tonight, we find our pleasure, Edwina. Tomorrow, we can war."

She felt as though a great weight had lifted—the weight of her responsibility to herself to resist. As though something broke inside her, warmth rushed through her. The promise in his eyes was seductive. He made pleasure seem possible. Even inevitable. She swallowed and gave him a nod.

His reaction was swift, a one-sided smile, an even more smoldering gaze. He scooted down the bed until his head hovered over one small breast. She slid her hand between them, covering it. He tugged her hand away then lowered, sticking out his tongue to stroke the nipple.

She gasped as her areola dimpled and the tip tightened. He aimed breath in a narrow stream, cooling the wet bud, then kissed it, sucking it into his mouth where he teased it with his tongue.

Heat swept over her skin. Gooseflesh prickled. Her legs moved restlessly, trapped by his weight as he moved to the other breast and renewed the sweet torture.

Her head thrashed, so many sensations bombarding her— the rasp of his beard, the pull of his lips, the liquid spilling from inside her... How had he brought her to arousal so quickly?

Again, he moved downward, his tongue tracing her ribs, dipping into her navel, then lower still. When his face was above her mound, she bowed upward in alarm. "What are you doing?"

"What I must," he said.

"'Tis sinful," she gasped as his tongue stroked her outer folds. Sinful, but oh so pleasurable.

He raised his head to give her a narrow stare. "You would

not have barred your gates against your husband if you feared Hell."

"I barred my gates against a barbarian, knowing God would understand."

He grunted and bent over her again, parting her with his fingers. Good Lord, why was he looking there? She slipped her hand between them to cup her sex. "I am already wet. You have accomplished what you sought. You can enter me now."

His head shook, as did his chest. Was he laughing at her? With her free hand, she sank her fingers in his hair and pulled. But he would not be dislodged. He pulled away her hand, and his mouth burrowed between her folds; his tongue stroked her entrance.

"Sinful," she whispered. But, oh, it was also glorious. Her hips bucked when his thumb rasped across the sensitive knot at the top of her folds. "Oh, please, please stop." But her hands clutched his hair, pulling her to him, anchoring him there, because now, she was desperate for the release his efforts promised.

When his lips latched around her hard knot, she whimpered. When two of his thick fingers entered her, she bucked. But he held her still, drawing hard on her knot, fingers pumping inside her. Her back arched and she cried out, darkness closing around her vision.

When she came back to herself, he was kneeling between her thighs.

She waited, spellbound, as he came over her and began to push inside her.

Although she was wet, her quim burned as he stretched her, shallow thrusts breaching her then sinking deeper with each steady forward push. She slid up her heels on the mattress, curving her hips to accept his thrusts. Glancing between them, she watched, fascinated with the sight of his thick shaft disappearing inside her. Tension built inside her womb again.

Passion tightened his cheeks. A deep flush was spreading there. His eyes were losing their focus, becoming smokier, his lids falling. He was finding pleasure, intense pleasure, if the quivering of his arms and shoulders was any indication.

And suddenly she felt powerful, no longer the conquered one. Her own motives began to disintegrate beneath the blistering heat they built. There was pleasure in surrender, but it went both ways.

"Stop," she whispered.

He went still, his gaze falling to her face. Slowly he pulled free of her. His chest billowed around deep breaths, and he held himself on his arms above her. "Did I cause you pain?" he asked, his voice hoarse.

She shook her head. Then without saying a word, she reached down and slid her fingers around the base of his cock, all the while marveling at the thickness, the steel-like firmness wrapped in warm, supple skin. She pulled him forward, fit his head against her entrance then glanced up to meet his gaze. "I am not sorry I barred my gates to you."

He held still, studying her face.

"Had we met in a normal fashion, I would have dismissed you as I have a dozen suitors before you. I have had little respect or need for a man. And I suppose my first husband spoiled something inside me."

His eyes closed for a moment, and then he speared her with a hot look. "I will never dishonor your trust in me. I will never strike you. You know these lands and your people. I will listen to your counsel."

Her eyes filled, knowing they were speaking their private

vows. That this was the true consummation of their union. "I will honor you. I will *try* never to disagree with you in public, and I will trust you with my property as I will trust you with my body." And then she offered him a smile. Her first.

His smile was warm and beautiful as he entered her. And this time, there was no discomfort, no burning, just a luscious fullness that spread upward, filling her chest with hope for their shared future. This burly knight, this dark barbarian, was only a man who wished a home. A place of his own. Well, perhaps he only wanted the respect and stature being lord of the keep would bring, but wasn't it her role to make him appreciate the other things she brought?

Starting now. She raised her head and bit his shoulder, hoping she hadn't read him wrongly.

His swift, tight smile was followed by a blazing glare. He captured her hands, drawing them up and together, holding them easily as she writhed beneath him, her movements seeming to incite him. His own measured thrusts grew harsher, deeper, and she reveled in the violence, meeting his darkening gaze with a narrowed one of her own.

"Our passions are well matched," he growled.

She jutted her chin, unwilling to bend enough to agree.

Abruptly, he pulled free. In an instant, he rolled her, forcing her with his hard hands to her knees. His cock nudged her entrance then thrust, impaling her, and she groaned, coming up on her arms and twisting to give him a quelling stare.

His laughter filled the air, and she turned toward the wall to hide her own grin. Their lovemaking was becoming a contest. One she found she relished.

A smack landed on her backside, and her quim tightened around him even as a fresh wash of fluid drenched his cock.

With a glide of his finger on her small nubbin, she went rigid, pleasure exploding.

Moments later, he gave a shout. His motions slowed, then stopped. They both hung there, their bodies still connected, ragged breaths punctuating the air.

A kiss landed on her shoulder. His face nuzzled into the corner of her neck. "Well played, milady."

She shook her head, no dismay creeping in to sour the moment. "You have won, it seems."

A chuckle shook her. Rather than withdraw, he held her hips as he brought them to the mattress then spooned his body around hers. She rested on his thick upper arm, inhaling the scent of sex, his musk, surrounded by the man. Captured. In his thrall. And happily so.

The next morning, Grimvarr held her hand as they entered the hall. Lord Alred was already seated on the dais breaking his fast. Everyone stared as the couple crossed to take their places at the head table.

She knew what they saw. Her cheeks were still rosy from having awakened with him hard and sliding inside her. His face bore the expression of a man who had been well pleasured. Together, they exuded an aura of sensual ease. They were lovers.

Geade glanced up from his table and raised his glass, a silent toast. Relief was apparent in his smile.

Grimvarr made a show of helping her take her seat then lifted her hand from her lap, turned it and kissed her palm. Edwina's eyes filled at the tender gesture. Still bent over her hand, Grimvarr offered her a smile, one filled with wicked promise.

Beside her, Lord Alred lifted his beaker of mulled wine. "To a glorious siege!"

WICKED

Susannah Chapin

Stirling Castle, Scotland, 1707 AD

Most castle inhabitants spoke of him in hushed tones as though he were an apparition. Since returning from battle with an axe wound to the leg, Lachlan had barely walked among the living. In truth, even before he left for battle, he skirted the edges of society. Maybe that was what drew Isobell to the warrior who had led her father's army since she was little more than a child.

Her mother said he was a lost cause. Some whispered he wasn't right in the head. That he was dangerous. Others claimed he was deviant. Wicked. Isobell dismissed those rumors. All that really mattered was that whatever he was, she would do anything for him.

She crept into his bedchamber, overwhelmed by the smell of peat smoke, urine and male musk.

Lachlan sprawled on his stomach, his black hair curling over his ears. Even in sleep, deep grooves furrowed his brow, and she longed to smooth them away. His nose had been broken since she last saw him, the knot of scar tissue thicker than before.

Still, he was the most beautiful man she'd ever seen.

Broken, but beautiful. So different from her dead husband.

She kindled the fire and tidied the room, the activity pressing her fears to the back of her mind. Whether she was more afraid of being caught in Lachlan's room past midnight or of what would happen if she weren't, she didn't know or care. She was there for one thing only—to bring this man back from the dead.

The growing fire warmed the room and Lachlan moaned, turning onto his back, the covers draping over his hips, a thick thigh exposed. His broad chest, covered with dark hair, rose and fell with his breaths.

Drawing near, Isobell feasted on the taut lines of his belly, the thin line of hair disappearing beneath the sheet, and lower to the angry twisted scar bisecting his thigh from groin to knee.

Her gasp was soft but not soft enough. In a motion so fast Isobell didn't have time to scream, Lachlan pinned her to the wall, his massive forearm across her chest and a dirk at her throat. Panic gripped her in its iron fist, her shallow breaths doing nothing to tame her blackening vision.

He was going to kill her.

As quickly as the fury came, it receded, recognition dawning across Lachlan's steel-gray eyes. "Isobell?" His voice was ragged with disuse. "Christ, what are ye doing here?"

She swallowed hard as the dirk's cool blade left her skin. Trembling fingers flew to her neck, her elbow grazing his naked torso. Her heartbeat pounded in her ears, and a sheen of cold sweat dotted her face and chest.

There was barely a hairbreadth between his naked body and

hers. His masculine scent wrapped around her, drowning her in desire.

She gathered her nerve, squared her shoulders and peered up at him. "I'm here to bring ye back."

"Is it yer da? Does he need me?" He reached to the side for his plaid draped over a chair, ready in a heartbeat to serve her father. Never a moment's fear or doubt, just unshakable loyalty, bone-deep bravery.

Isobell reached to still his fingers with hers. "Nay, it isna my da."

He straightened, towering over her. Long and lean, built for power and speed. A deadly combination of brains and brawn. Confusion knit his brow. "Then why are ye here? Ye shouldna be sneaking around the castle at night."

Her practiced speeches were tendrils of fog she couldn't quite grasp under his icy gaze. What had she planned to say? *Use me in any way necessary to feel alive again?* What manner of idiot was she?

"Isobell." He touched her chin, tipping it until she met his eyes.

Something dark and liquid pooled in her belly.

"I think ye should leave now, lass," he said, his voice tinged with anger.

She stiffened her back, grasped the fleeing strings of her frayed courage and infused her tone with all the authority she could muster. "I brought ye water and soap. There's a clean shirt and food, too. Wash up and I'll change yer sheets." She brushed past him and stripped the sheets, the weight of his gaze on her.

Water splashed in the basin just before he spoke. "Leave the sheets. I'll do the bed."

"Nay. Let me tend ye." Isobell avoided his nakedness as she dumped the dirty bedclothes outside the chamber door. She'd give him privacy. For now.

"I dinna need tending, lass," he said, irritation in his curt words. "I'm a grown man, ye ken?"

The edge in his tone was sharp enough to sever her tender resolve, but Isobell refused to bleed. "I'm not sure of that. It didna look like ye were caring of yerself, sleeping in filth and refusing to leave yer room."

"And what would ye know of it?" he spat.

"I know ye lay in here, day and night. I know ye stopped riding, stopped hunting. Ye pay the maids to bring yer food but won't let them help ye wash. Ye came back from battle a ghost of who ye were." She paused, her fingers bunching in the fresh sheets. "The most frightening part is that ye were little more than a ghost when ye left. Ye're ashamed of yer leg, of yer limp, so ye push everyone away. People talk about ye, Lachlan. They whisper things."

The heat of him pressed against her back. His warm breath caressed her neck as he spoke low and deadly. "And what do they say about me, sweet Bell? Tell me, so I can show ye how true it is."

A shiver skittered down her spine, not of fear, but need. "They say..." Isobell swallowed hard and tried again. "They say ye want things. In bed. Strange things."

The rough pads of Lachlan's fingers caught on the soft linen of her nightgown as his hand splayed over her stomach, pulling her against his chest. Her breath hitched as his lips grazed her ear.

"And yet ye're here, sweet Bell." His chuckle was as dangerous as the man himself. Thick fingers wove through her hair and tugged her head to the side. "Such bawdy talk. Are ye as bawdy as ye are beautiful? Did ye talk this way wi' yer man?"

She was sure he intended to make her run, to conjure thoughts of bedding a dead and buried Angus lost to illness two winters before. But it wouldn't work.

"We never talked." Isobell cleared her throat. "In the bedroom. He took what he needed and that was that."

She wouldn't tell more. Not how Angus needed to strike her or place his hand around her throat in order to get hard. Those secrets were best left buried with the man.

A loaded silence stretched between them before Lachlan spoke. "My bedchamber is no place for ye." He released her hair and stepped away. "Thank ye for the bath and the food. It'd be best if ye left."

Isobell scrambled for words and turned to him. "I'm not leaving."

Lachlan's eyes traveled down her body, lingering on her breasts and hips. "Isobell, I've known ye since ye were born. What do ye want from me?"

Heart pounding, Isobell lifted her chin. "I want ye to use me."

It was impossible to miss the way his massive frame twitched on the word *use*. His smoky eyes branded her; his fists clenched. His breaths were as labored as hers. "This is a dangerous game ye're playing. Leave now, before the stakes are too high."

"They're already too high." She raised her face, letting him see her need. "Do ye not know how I feel for ye? How it breaks me to see ye this way?"

"Go. Please. I dinna need yer pity."

He tried to hide his emotions behind a scowl, but Isobell knew better. "No, Lachlan. I've wanted ye since I was a girl."

She reached for the tie of her nightgown. "Let me give ye this. Please."

He crossed the space between them in two long, limping steps, and his hands stilled hers. "Isobell," he whispered. "I can't...this isna right."

Tears stung her eyes. "Ye don't want me?"

His forehead touched hers, eyes closed, mouth pressed into a thin line. "I do. Christ, yes, I do. I have for too long, my sweet Bell."

"Then give this to me. Please."

His breath warmed her face as he warred with himself. Finally his gaze met hers, heat for heat. "Tell me what ye like. What ye want."

Victory. She wouldn't give him time to change his mind. "I want ye to kiss me," she blurted.

Lachlan cradled her face, thumbs tracing her eyebrows and cheeks. One moved to her lips, his gaze fixed there as it caressed the curves. "Ye're so beautiful."

When his lips touched hers, it wasn't in the hungry way she'd expected but a gentle brushing, a tease. Isobell moaned and wrapped her arms around his shoulders. "More," she said.

And he obliged, angling his head to take her mouth. She opened to him, nails digging into the skin of his back. A low sound in the back of his throat signaled the loosening of his tightly reined control, and his tongue plundered her mouth.

The sweet heat of him licking into her mouth drove her wild. Her already slippery sex grew swollen and fevered, aching to feel him.

Isobell fisted his hair and guided his mouth over hers. He crushed her to him, hard cock pressing into her belly. He wanted her, needed her as desperately as she needed him.

It was a heady feeling, to be wanted so. She'd felt like nothing more than a warm body with Angus, a soft hole to be filled. But not with Lachlan. She had the distinct feeling that, held between his two hands, she was something to be cherished.

"Tell me what ye want," he repeated.

"I want to see ye."

Hesitance flashed in his eyes and made her heart ache.

"I don't care about the scars." She traced a wide, flat scar on his chest that looked as though he'd been flayed. "They're a part of who ye are. And that makes them beautiful." She pressed a kiss over his heart and reached for the cloth around his hips.

His breath caught as the material fell away, his cock springing to attention.

Isobell had a similar reaction to his perfection, and her sex squeezed, hungry for his touch. She gorged herself on the sight of him: his hard chest and lean stomach, the delicate, creamy white skin of his belly, and the thick nest of dark curls surrounding his cock.

He was big. Much larger than she had ever seen. At the tip, a drop of moisture glistened in the firelight.

When she glanced up, his gaze was downcast in shame. Or maybe...deference?

Isobell stroked the soft skin of his upper thigh, and he shuddered. "Lachlan? Look at me."

His eyes met hers without hesitation, raw and hungry.

"Ye are magnificent." Her fingers grazed his balls, and they drew up toward his body as he gasped.

His breaths became harsh pants. "Let me..." He swallowed hard. "Let me serve ye, Bell. Tell me how."

Steeling her nerve, she untied the laces and let her nightgown fall.

He drank her in, eyes fevered. "Christ, Bell," he said, voice thick. "Please. Tell me."

"Kiss me. Kiss my body."

He was on her in an instant, uncertainty forgotten. The backs of her knees hit the bed, and they tumbled onto the fresh sheets. She expected him to flip her onto her stomach, to push into her with a grunt and a slap to her arse.

But he didn't.

Instead, he began at her mouth, kissing her until she was breathless. He traced her neck, the soft skin where it met her shoulder, the sweep of her collarbone. Goose bumps chased his exploring fingers, and Bell longed to feel that touch everywhere.

It would be such a simple thing for him to move on top of her, spread her thighs and slide inside. And she craved that from him, but something told her that he wouldn't. Not unless she told him to.

His lips whispered over her eyes, and she sighed. They moved down to kiss the hollow behind her ear, his tongue, hot and wet, gliding over that sensitive spot. She arched against him and clasped his hair in a tight fist, eliciting a moan from deep in his throat.

His head lifted, eyes searching hers for permission. "Please, tell me how I can please ye." His voice was a ragged whisper, drowning under the strain of need.

"I...I don't know." She knew how to pleasure herself, but had no idea how to direct a man.

"Ye have...ye have to tell me."

She expected him to be commanding and insistent, but he wasn't. He was uncertain and gentle, in need of guidance.

"Touch me. Kiss me more. *Everywhere*."

There was no hesitation. His lips surrounded her nipple with wet heat. Pleasure burst through her, sizzling directly to her sex, and Isobell clawed his shoulders. As her nails carved crescents in his skin, Lachlan's hips bucked, his choked inhalation muffled by her breast.

"Oh Christ, Bell," he panted, moving to the other breast. His fingers found her wet nipple, rolled it, and a fresh surge of wetness slicked her sex.

He pressed kisses down her body, dipped his tongue into the well of her navel, before coming to her triangle of curls. He pushed her legs apart.

Yes! Isobell thought. *This is it.* She ached for him to fill her with his cock.

But Lachlan didn't push into her. Instead, he settled between her thighs, face inches from her sex.

Isobell dug her heels into the bed, tried to scramble away, but his big hands were on her hips; the muscles in his arms knotted, as unyielding as her desire. He dragged her back down, his warm breaths gusting over her slickness.

"I would like to." He stopped, cleared his throat. "I'd like to make ye feel good. Will ye let me?"

"H-How?"

"I'd like to kiss ye. Here." His fingers traced her wet seam, and her hips jerked. "May I?"

"Do people *do* that?"

Lachlan chuckled, deep and dark. "Aye. They do."

Even his breath against that oversensitized spot was bliss. Isobell couldn't imagine what his mouth would feel like.

She barely had time to nod when his thumbs slid through her lips, spreading them for his inspection, and her cheeks flamed.

Without warning, his tongue circled her nubbin, and sensation blazed from that spot to spike her blood with pure need. With a cry, Isobell grasped his hair again. The touch lit something inside Lachlan, and his mouth opened to devour her sex. His beard rasped her sensitive flesh while he kissed between her legs just as he had kissed her mouth, causing the desire in her belly to coil tightly.

Big hands cupped her arse and tipped her to his mouth, giving him better access. When his tongue dipped inside her, she bucked against his face, shivering as her climax drew closer.

"Ah, Christ. Yer quim is so sweet," he murmured against her swollen flesh.

He was doing this to her. With his mouth. He suckled her hard little knot, slid two long fingers inside her, and the tightly coiled thing sprung free. She climaxed against Lachlan's face, his hand, with a strangled cry.

Lachlan nuzzled her thigh as she recovered. "Did I please ye?"

"Aye, ye did," she said, gasping, forcing her breaths to slow. "Now it's yer turn."

He sat back on his haunches, face veiled. "Nay, ye let me please ye. That's enough."

He was hard as rock, his shaft ridged with vicious veins, the head a livid purple. So why was he denying her?

She sat up and wrapped his cock in a tight fist.

"Bell, this isna... Please." He swallowed.

Isobell rose to her knees in front of him, ran her hands over his chest, his shoulders, down the corded muscles of his arms. She pinched his nipples between her thumbs and forefingers, and he sucked in a breath, his gaze lowering and cock twitching.

Color stained his cheeks. A rough hand in his hair, the scrape of her nails, a roll of his nipples. *Tell me what to do.* Lachlan needed her to take charge, needed to receive pain just as Angus had liked to give it. And it shamed him.

"Look at me," Isobell commanded, and his gaze darted to hers. "I will have ye tonight, Lachlan McKenzie."

"Bell."

"Aye, that's right. Beg me, but not to stop, because I won't."

"I canna…"

Something feral bubbled up inside Isobell, and she wrapped her hand around Lachlan's throat.

He shuddered, and a low moan vibrated against her palm.

"I said beg me."

Lachlan swallowed against her tightening hand. He met her eyes, his filled with doubt and shame.

She pulled him to her for a kiss, invading his mouth.

With a groan, his arms banded around her body and pulled her onto his lap.

Isobell whispered against his lips, "It's okay, Lachlan. I know what ye need. Let me be this for ye."

He searched her eyes, his gray ones uncertain. "Ye don't…" He paused, took a deep breath. "Ye don't think me a pervert? I don't make ye sick?"

The words were more painful than any physical blow. She cupped his cheek. "Nay, Lachlan. I dinna think that. I think ye're a man wi' needs and I want verra much to fulfill them. Ye dinna make me sick; ye make me feel good. Happy. Safe. I want to make ye feel the same."

The tension melted from his shoulders.

Her hand slid to his throat once more, and she pushed him flat to the bed. "Now beg me."

"Please, please will ye use me?" His voice shook, body trembling with need.

"Use ye how?" Her free hand explored the sculpted lines of his abdomen, the hard mass of his chest, the deep V of the muscles that cut from hip to groin. He was so solid, so strong. A warrior. The hands that held her with tenderness had no mercy for the countless men he'd killed in battle. He could hunt and fight and survive the wilderness. She'd once seen him snap the neck of a wolf with his bare hands. He was an island of carefully reined power, commanding respect and awe.

But here, with her, he was something else. He needed to give up the tightly leashed control and be at someone else's mercy. Her mercy. It was a heady feeling to give him what no one else could, to see a part of him that he kept hidden.

"For yer pleasure," he said.

"And what else?"

"Hurt me," he whispered.

Isobell chewed her lip, her self-doubt floating to the surface. It didn't take long for her need to please Lachlan to outweigh any misgivings. She landed a smack to his uninjured thigh. "Roll over."

He obeyed. The muscles of his back rippled as he settled himself on his stomach. Isobell's eyes wandered to his perfect arse, the round mass of muscle lightly dusted in fine hair. She leaned forward and sunk her teeth into the taut flesh.

Lachlan moaned.

"Ye have a verra fine arse, Lachlan," Isobell mused. "It's verra fair. Except here." She raked her fingernails over the indentations she left in his skin, and he shivered. With a wicked grin, she bit his other buttock, sucking the flesh, marveling at the livid red mark she left behind.

Lachlan writhed beneath her.

"Don't squirm," she commanded before landing a solid blow to his arse with her open hand. He gasped, and she struck him again. A rapid succession of equally brutal blows left his cheeks glowing brilliant red and hot to the touch. The curve of his spine glistened with sweat, and his massive ribs expanded with labored breaths.

"Get up on yer knees." When he tried to straighten his arms, an elbow in the center of his back had him presenting with his arse in the air and chest resting on his forearms. Isobell traced the raised ridges her spanking left on his buttocks. When one finger strayed close to the seam between his cheeks, Lachlan cried out, his hips bucking and arse clenching.

Inspired, Isobell ran a finger through the cleft. When she reached his puckered hole, Lachlan hissed a breath and tried to move away. "No, Lachlan. Stay right there."

Bell circled his arsehole with a fingertip. He was shuddering, his breaths coming in great gusts. Nudging his knees apart, Bell moved between them, and his shaking intensified. With only a moment of self-doubt, she spit between his cheeks.

"Oh Jesus Christ. Oh Lord. Did ye just..." He trailed off with a groan.

Feeling deliciously evil, she leaned forward and thrust two fingers into his mouth, swirling them around until they were wet. He groaned when she pulled away, then cried out when she worked one into his arsehole.

He cursed, his hips working back onto her exploring finger. "Oh Jesus, Bell. That's...oh God."

He was so soft and warm, so tight that she couldn't help but work another finger inside. His body quaked, breath ragged, a sheen of sweat glossing his back. Bell leaned down to trace the marks on his arse with her tongue as she fucked him with her fingers.

"I can't. Bell. I can't hold on wi' ye doin' that." His voice was a choked whisper.

"Aye, ye can and ye will." She grasped his cock in her fist. His hips lurched forward, fucking her hand, and Bell suppressed her own moan even as Lachlan gave in to his.

His swollen cock pulsed and jerked in her palm. He was so slick at the tip, so ready to come.

"Isobell, please. It's too good."

She withdrew her fingers. "Tell me what ye want, then."

"I want to feel ye around me," he said, his voice hoarse. "I want to make ye feel this good."

Her greedy hand left his cock and yanked his head back. "Ye'll do what I ask?"

"Yes, anything."

"Good. Fuck me hard."

He turned and lunged full force, pinning her on her back, his hips wedged between her thighs. His cock was a weapon poised to strike. He groaned and gripped his shaft, parting her flushed folds with the smooth, swollen head.

Bell gasped as he stretched her, the burn a precious ache that she would cherish for the rest of her days.

Lachlan's eyes squeezed shut, arms trembling. "Bell. Ye amaze me, love."

"Open yer eyes, Lachlan," she said. His lashes fluttered and gray pools of utter devotion hit her with the force of a blow to the chest. "Watch what ye do to me."

Lachlan's eyes were glassy, dreamy, as though he were disappearing into a fantasy. Bell needed him with her. And to bring him back to her, to them, she landed a slap across his face that left her palm stinging and the imprint of her hand branding his cheek. He moaned low in his throat, his eyes drifting to hers, heavy lidded and drunk on pleasure.

Isobell felt drunk, as well. Drunk on power, on the ability to bring this man to his knees. She didn't want it to end. Now that she had a taste of Lachlan, she couldn't bear to go back.

Lachlan's thrusts grew faster, deeper. His clean sweat and male musk surrounded her, tied her up in him.

"I canna hold on, love. Ye're so tight. So wet."

"Not yet." She was so close.

His hand found her hip, angled it so his cock rubbed some secret place inside her, fingers digging hard enough to bruise, and Isobell came. She clawed at his shoulder as she rode the waves of pleasure, her quim milking his cock. Above her, those steely eyes pleaded for release.

Her voice was raw when she spoke. "Come, Lachlan. Let me feel ye let go."

Relief washed over him as he came; his lips parted in pleasure so blinding that no sound could be made; his face was painted with awe. Long moments later, he collapsed, his weight a solid comfort pinning her to the bed, to the perfection of the moment.

Too soon, he pulled out and rolled them to their sides, cradling Isobell against his shoulder. "I dinna know what to say." He pressed a kiss to the top of her head. "But I never expected that."

"Are ye sorry? For what we did?"

He chuckled, the years disappearing from his face. "Nay, my Bell. As long as I live, I'll never regret that. But I doubt I'll live long if yer da hears what I've done. At least I'll die a verra happy man."

Tears stung the backs of her eyes. "Dinna talk about dying, Lachlan McKenzie," she said more forcefully than she intended.

His hands cupped her face, eyes searching hers. "Hey, lass. What's amiss? I was only teasing."

Her gaze dropped to his chest, voice a tight whisper. "I thought ye dead when they brought ye in from battle. I thought ye gone and..." She trailed off as the tears fell.

He tipped her chin, studied her face, eyes imploring her to finish.

"I wanted to die, too," she whispered.

He crushed her to his chest. "Oh, Bell, my love. What are ye sayin'?"

"I don't want to live without ye. I can't." She molded her body to his, reveling in his heat, his size, his smell, all the things that made him strong and male and *him*.

He pushed her back enough to see her face. "Are ye saying ye love me?"

Tears fell anew, and she choked out a laugh. "Ye must think me daft, loving ye all my life and never saying a word."

He shook his head. "Nay, I dinna think ye daft. I think ye bonny and brave and smart and so, so sweet." He punctuated each word with a kiss to her salty cheeks. "And mine. I think ye're mine."

"Aye, I am yers. I love ye."

"As I love ye, my Bell. I have for too long, and for too long I've done nothing about it. I know..." He trailed off, eyes straying to his maimed leg. "I know I dinna have much to offer ye, but I swear if ye'll have me, I'll give ye all I have. The protection of my hands and my sword, the use of my body to pleasure ye, and all of my heart. Forever."

Isobell's heart swelled in her chest until she could barely breathe. "Aye, I'll have ye, Lachlan. All of ye."

He claimed her mouth and settled between her thighs again.

She grinned up at him. "Now all ye have to do is tell my da."

His smile lit the room like the sunrise that would sneak through the window in mere hours. But they had time. All the time in the world. "Ye're a wicked, wicked woman, Isobell."

She hid her smirk behind a bitten lip and grasped his cock. "And ye like it."

He laughed, pressing a kiss to her lips. "Aye, I do. And I wouldna have ye any other way."

The Keeper
of the Keys

Axa Lee

County Kent, Britain, 452 AD

I clench beneath his hands, sweated up and lathered as a mare. Instead of his hand landing on my ass again, it goes to my hair, brushing back the sweat-damp swath of auburn mane from my face, while he's murmuring along my ear as though I were a horse to be soothed and caressed. Under his hands, I relax.

He's speaking the barbarian Saxon tongue, so I only catch one word in ten. I'm not really trying though. Once in a while I catch a Latin phrase, or something in Greek, meaning basically the same as what I think he's saying in his own language, "Shh. Easy, girl. Relax. Good girl, gooood girl."

And his hand comes down again, a solid, thrilling blow to the meat of my ass. The weight of the blow sinks in, reddening my cheeks and heating a path all the way to my cunt. The blows are glorious. He holds my wrists behind my back with one hand, while with the other he spanks and grips, or thrusts his rough warrior's fingers into my well-lubricated slit. Nothing gets me as wet as when I'm completely at his mercy, his muscled thighs supporting me, my breasts bouncing down, ass thrust in the air. It's the only time I'm not in charge.

Outside our small thatched hut, the snow falls, another harsh winter brewing. But here, beside our hearth, with the cook pot suspended on a chain over the fire, I have laid my household keys aside with a clink, along with my brooches, and I have lain bare to this taciturn man who I claimed for a husband.

I groan under his hand, arching my back, ready to come, *aching* to come.

"You're a lusty wench, aren't you?" he says, in rough Briton. He's been learning our language, since no one in the village will lower themselves to speak Saxon. They might understand it perfectly well, but, when it's spoken to them by those who've invaded our lands, filling the hole of power left in my grandfather's time by the retreating Roman legions, they'll give the speaker a sullen look and reply in the fewest words possible.

I bite my lip in response, but a low moan of pleasure escapes when his hand meets my flesh, three times in quick succession—one cheek, the other, and back to the first. I'm trembling again, craving his cock, craving release, but craving this giving up of responsibility more.

He stoked the fire before we began, so the thickening of smoke before it escapes through the hole in the roof chokes me a little, promising a sore throat. He's turned my back toward the fire, so my ass is even hotter while my head remains cooler. It makes for a startling sensation. My nipples are rigid in the chill while my bottom burns.

His hand comes down again and I clench, then shudder. He

grabs a handful of my ass, grunting at the meat and heft of it before releasing the cheek to sink his fingers deep into my wet slit. He purposefully hits the spot deep inside that makes me gasp, bucking against his hand. He pulls out just as I'm about to come, leaving me shaking across his knees.

"Not yet, beauty," he says, smoothing back the wild tangle of hair from my face. "Not yet."

It's the only time I let him take charge like this. Ever since I can remember the household keys have hung from my belt. They are the first thing I reach for in the morning and the last thing I check at night. The day I served ale to the Saxon warriors who'd ridden into our village, demanding food and drink, and settled on which warlord I would marry, the keys weighed heavy against my thigh, reminding me of the weight of my obligation to my people. Since the retreat of the legions, we'd been waiting for the invaders to reach our remote village.

"Barbarians will come to these shores," my pragmatic father told me. Not long after he rode away to war against those barbarians and never returned. "They respect only might and blood. Remote as we are, they will find us, and when they do you must marry one of them."

And so I did. Cutha, son of Eadger, a Saxon chief with his ragged war band. Cutha had been rewarded with our lands for his service to his chief...if he could conquer us. With his few warriors, Cutha, already in disgrace, was not expected to succeed. They rode in, expecting a fight, and were met with hospitality instead of war.

"I will wed with you," I'd told him. I'd drawn him to a relatively secluded alcove of the mead hall, pressing his back against the wall and the knife that hung from my belt against his groin. "And these lands and wealth will bring you prestige and a place in government among your own people. But in the day to day, my word will be law. You will obey and abide by my decisions. If this is not acceptable, if you seek to seize power from me or raise arms against me or my people, we will set fire to the land and salt the earth and leave nothing but devastation in our wake. We will abide, but we will not bow. Are those terms acceptable?"

He'd studied me with blue eyes as pale as springwater. He saw the iron in me at that moment, he told me later, the resolve that if I could not keep control of my lands, then no one else would have them either. He told me later he fell in love with me then, with my hard mouth and flinty eyes, softened by the passion flaring my nose.

"My lady," he'd said, and kissed my ring finger as though I were a king.

A shiver had run up my arm, culminating in a moment of pleasure deep within me. I pulled my hand away, more sharply than I meant, and suppressed the rush of desire I felt.

And so a man with nothing to lose met a woman who stood to lose everything, who would do anything to save it.

Cutha's hand comes down again, bouncing a little, stinging. I grit my teeth as chills run all over my body, setting every hair to attention.

"Power is isolating," my father had told me, "power is lonely."

My husband's cock is hardening against my belly. It feels so strange this way, the shaft bouncing across my ribs instead of pressing from beneath them. I'd like to take it in my mouth, run my tongue along his hardened shaft, roll his balls with my tongue. But he'd have to let me move, and he has no intention of that. He spanks again, next skewering my cunt on two crossed fingers. I clench around him, crying out, hips thrusting. He pulls out and the sting of his hand across the flesh of my ass stays me a little.

"Not yet, beauty," he says, stroking back my hair as I'm shaking, panting.

Our married life had quickly assumed a routine, much like that I'd enjoyed before. I rose before dawn to stir the fire and heat food from our meal the night before to break our fast. Next came the fetching of water and the milking. By then Cutha would rise and set to bringing wood in for the fire. After seeing that our fire would last the day, he left with the other men, to plant, plow, or harvest in the spring and summer months, hunt wolves or chop wood in the winter. Sometimes we barely spoke to each other for days.

I'd always worked hard, but during this time it seemed I worked harder than ever—checking the grain stores for rodent damage; supervising and taking my turn at the carding, spinning and weaving; asking into the brewing; checking the cheese processing; lending a hand to the milking; making sure the children and their dogs were accounted for, along with the cattle and sheep; that the men had put by enough firewood to see us through a bad winter storm; that the smith had enough iron and the potter enough clay; all the little things that kept a steading running smoothly. Not to mention the daily tasks of cooking, cleaning, mending, laundering, settling disputes, issuing orders and punishments. I made sure we had enough grain, stock and iron to pay the tribute every year when Cutha and I traveled to the cyning's seat along the eastern shore to pledge our loyalty. And I made sure my husband was satisfied when he took his pleasure of me, and I of him.

But when I collapsed on my pallet at night, though Cutha lay beside me and all my needs were met, I felt beaten down by exhaustion and loneliness, a sense of isolation that I could not identify.

It began with a rap of his knuckles over my ass. I'd bent over the fire, to stir the pottage for supper. I'd been nattering at my husband again, something I'd become acutely aware of, cringing whenever I heard my own voice. Cutha had been working alongside the other men in the village all day and yet when he came in, exhausted, and sat down to eat, I kept at him, asking for this chore and that.

When had I become this harsh, shrewish person? The unsatisfied wife from all the stories?

I was midsentence about the cleaning out from beneath where the chickens roost when he rapped my ass with his knuckles, saying, "I'm a warrior. Not a chicken herder. Feed me, woman, and stop nattering. I'll get to it."

It was one of those moments that really didn't matter much to him. I doubt he even remembered it later. But it made a great impression upon me. Because while he'd struck my ass, it was my cunt that responded, the liquid heat spreading, making my nether lips slicken and swell as I struggled to catch my breath and make my head cease wheeling.

When we lay down beside each other on our pallet next to the fire that night, I shifted, restless.

"What is wrong?" Cutha asked finally, voice terse. Not from temper with me, I learned, but from his struggle with our language.

I didn't want to say, and yet I couldn't not, not when my cunt dripped at the very thought of his big warrior's hand connecting with my bare flesh, slapping, squeezing. Already, the imagined scenario had me shaking, my head spinning with the possibilities.

"What you did earlier..." The darkness made me bold. "With your knuckles, could you...do that again?"

In the glow from the banked fire, I saw confusion cloud his eyes for a moment before they cleared with understanding. He took a moment to reply, during which I began to panic that he would turn away from me, disgusted.

"This thing you ask," he said slowly as snakes of doubt coiled in my belly, "is not a thing to undertake lightly. You must wait."

"How long?" I was still on the verge of panic, thinking that he was putting me off indefinitely. It was then I noticed the corners of his mouth quirking upward as he bit back amusement at my overeagerness. He made a male noise of lust and reached around me, hauling me against him so I could feel his arousal, long and hard against my thigh. He cupped my ass with one of his big warrior's hands, kneading roughly, while he kissed ever so gently along my neck. I barely recognized the surprised exclamations of pleasure that escaped my lips. They were sounds I'd never known myself to make before.

"Patience," he said. His hand slipped down to cup my sex, one finger searching through my lower curls to find my wet center. "You're sopping, beauty," he said, and thrust the finger into me.

I cried out, clutching him, rocking against his hand as he worked inside me. When he brought me to the verge of bliss, he withdrew his hand and brought it down with a crack on my ass. I clung to him. He ran his hands over me, soothing my vibrating flesh with wordless nonsense, biting my ear with his lips and holding me against him.

44

"Soon, lovely," he said. "Soon."

Why this? I asked myself. Why now? And what would he think of me? Was he offering this pleasure merely because I asked or did he feel aroused by it too? Judging by the rigidity of his cock, this last was a stupid question. But it did make me realize how little I knew of him, and how I desired to know more. When we lay together that night, after he'd finished teasing me, I asked him, "Why did you agree to marry me?"

"You are the way to the land," he said. "Isn't that enough?"

"You could have had the land another way. Killed me, passed me off to your men. Why didn't you?"

"Dead peasants are of no use to me," he said. "Your people would have rebelled if I'd killed or disgraced you. I would have had to put the whole village to the sword, find new peasants, tramp down rebellion until you were dust and forgotten or until a lucky Briton arrow or blade found me. This way," he shrugged, his muscular shoulder rising and falling beneath my cheek, "life goes on as usual. And I get to bed down at night with a lusty wench." His hand found the core of me again, still wet, still easily making me gasp. He chuckled. "And you do not find me unpleasant either, I think."

"Other men would have taken the money and land and dispensed with me," I said, suddenly serious. "Or gotten a child on me within the year and laid claim to the land that way."

It was one of the unspoken things between us. It was not yet time for a child. We both knew that. It was one of the things I'd learned early to enjoy about him.

"My pleasure is in giving you pleasure," he'd explained shortly after we married. "I'd rather bring you pleasure a thousand times than myself once."

"I want you to enjoy yourself too though," I'd said.

"Believe me," he'd said with a groan. "I do." His mouth found mine, tender and hot. He teased my lips with his tongue and sunk a long finger into my slit.

"Other men," he'd said, turning over to lay nose to nose with me, "are fools."

I'd sighed into his mouth and he held me closer. I rolled my hips against his hand, urging him on. I could feel my mouth quivering against his as he stroked me, letting the pressure build inside me, making my pelvis ache with it. I arched my back, exclaiming as sensation rushed through me. The rushing of his breath beside my ear fed the flames of lust as they coursed through my veins. And then I couldn't hold it. I arched and cried out as the rush broke over me, sweeping through me in a torrent. His arms anchored me, one finger lingering on my clit until the spasms ceased. And when I opened my eyes, I was looking up into his, and the look on his face was raw and tender and possessive all at once.

"Fools," he'd whispered, and gathered me tightly against the heat of his body once more.

All the next day I couldn't concentrate. I saw to all the myriad details of the household, nodding as though I was listening to one complaint or another, while my other eye remained on my husband, seeking out Cutha wherever he was—mending harnesses, fetching water, chopping and carrying wood, or riding his warhorse out to check that the children had seen no wolves—and I bit my lip, wondering when I'd next feel his hands connecting with my flesh.

That night, as I prepared food, I was physically aware of him as I never had been. His seated form, muscular forearms braced against the rough plank of the wooden table, the casual

set of his shoulders—my skin prickled with his every movement, aching for him to reach for me, acutely aware of him
with every raised hair on my overly sensitive skin. But the night
wore on and he made no move for me, not until we lay down
to sleep, when he replayed the night before, hauling me against
him, alternating rough with tender, bringing me close to release
before withdrawing, and promising, "Soon, beauty, soon." For
three nights it played out this way, Cutha teasing me until I
nearly came, then soothing me back down, and we would talk
until we fell asleep.

I asked him about his home, about his family, about the
places he'd seen and the battles he'd won. He made me laugh,
and this surprised me. Few men had the power to make me
laugh. We spoke in Saxon, and Cutha seemed to relax as
he reminisced in his own language. He told me about the
service to his king that had resulted in his being gifted with
my land.

"I saved his life in battle, took an arrow meant for him."
Cutha showed me the scar, a puckered flesh wound at his
side. "And this one, where I stepped between Eathelred and
a swordsman. Luckily, the sword turned at the last moment."

I felt the divot the flat of the blade had left in his hairline.

"Knocked me out," he chuckled.

"If you saved him twice, why were you disgraced?"

"I spoke my mind."

And although it was nice because I was learning more about
my husband than I ever imagined, I still began to despair of his
ever satisfying me in the way that I'd asked.

But on the fourth night, this night, after supper, he rises,
pulls out the bench and begins stirring the fire, heating the room
to far warmer than we usually keep it. When he's finished, he

looks up at me, then taps the brooch at my shoulder that holds my woolens in place.

"This needs to come off," he says.

The shiver goes all the way from my shoulders to my pussy.

Almost shyly, I shed my clothes and stand before him, he still fully dressed and seated. He takes my hands and kisses the backs, then tugs me to stand between his knees. His hands move to my hips and his lips follow, kissing along the curve there.

I bite my lip, looking up at the roof. I feel one hand move and a moment later it smacks down on one of my asscheeks. I cry out, shocked from the blow and the pleasure washing through me after.

Cutha kneads my burning cheek and slowly bends me over his knees.

I am tense, uncertain what to expect. I needn't worry. We might have wed for convenience, this Saxon and I, but the gods had blessed me with an observant man with more than his share of tenderness.

He touches me everywhere, his hands freely roaming the expanse of my body, presented to him in a completely novel way. And it is then that reality sinks in and I quail, suddenly fearing he'll take this wrong, take it too far, hurt me more than I'm willing to be hurt. And just as I decide to rise, to tell him I've changed my mind, his hand lands squarely on my ass in a solid, smarting blow, and I am gone.

"You're a lusty wench, aren't you?" Cutha says in rough Briton.

I vibrate with the force of my arousal, shaking across his knees when he pulls his fingers from my pussy with a wet sucking sound, just as I am about to come.

"Not yet, beauty," he says, smoothing back the wild tangle of hair from my face. "Not yet."

He bends me over the table. His hand comes down with a crack now, sending pins and needles through me. The heat flows over my skin, pooling between my legs. I can feel the wetness, my wetness, spilling freely down my leg. The cry that escapes my throat is rough and raw, a half-tortured sound, ending in a wordless pleading for completion.

"Bring me, please, bring me, oh God, I need to come." I don't know if I say this or only think it, but Cutha gathers my meaning anyway.

"Touch yourself," he growls and bites my ear as he slides that thick, sweet cock into my gaping, wet hole. I do and am amazed at how full my nether lips are to the touch. I'm slick with the liquids of my desire. For this man, for this taciturn, kind, ambitious man.

And I'm coming, suddenly I'm coming, fingers dripping as they work my clitoris, his cock soaked and sliding in and out of me, hitting that magic place inside me that sets my entire body afire. I'm bursting inside, burning, spinning, falling, and the only thing reining me back is his voice, whispering beside my ear; his cock, pulsing inside me; his arms, wrapped around me.

"My queen," he says and kisses my ear. He draws me down on our pallet, his body curled protectively around mine, cock still buried deep inside me.

"Am I?" I whisper, breathless still.

He chuckles. "Since you first threatened my life." He squeezes me, exhaling a deeply male, deeply satisfied noise. "Are you well-served?" he asks.

And I think about it. Yes, I've been well fucked, and that's likely what he's asking. But if anything this experience has taught me that I need more. Before my thoughts coalesce enough to form a cohesive answer, he speaks again.

"I see you," he says. His voice is rough, but his hands are gentle. "You serve everyone. They all come to you, and you answer them. You care for them. You protect them. You married me to protect them. I married you because I will be cyning."

This surprises me. I had no idea he aspired to kingship. Though it makes sense, considering the views he'd expressed the past year or so about the current cyning.

"It will be a fight, but I am strong. *We*," he emphasizes this, "are strong."

He rolls me to my back to look up at him in the firelight, his blond hair a halo of flame. "I need a partner, an equal. Not just a wife and lover. And this is you, I think. Is this...what you think of me too?"

I study his face in the firelight. I see his intensity, his strength both of body and will, and I see his honesty. He isn't just talking about shared mutual appreciation or even passion. He is, I think, talking about love. Was that why I could yield to him, be vulnerable to him and no other? Do we have love? I think, perhaps, we do. We might.

"A consort," I say, "an equal, a lover?"

He nods.

My keys clink when my foot kicks them across the hut. As his laughter and arms encompass me, my ass is hot and my heart warm. He's mine, I know suddenly, with great clarity. And I am his. Perhaps we have love, but more than that we have respect, we have ambition, we have desire. And all I see are possibilities.

The Maiden's Kiss

Layla Chase

Thingvellir, Iceland, 950 AD

S moke hovered in a low cloud near the thatched roof of the long house hosting the meeting between neighboring clans. The scent of roasted great auk and puffin still lingered. A wooden bowl half-filled with clusters of golden-yellow cloudberries decorated the plank table.

Enar Hamarsen scraped his knife along the piece of tusk cradled in his palm, smoothing the flow of the chess piece's headdress. He'd left the queen until last. Anticipation proved important when appreciating a woman. Even a hard, cool, carved one. A calloused thumb smoothed over the scraping, testing for roughness. With the blade at an angle, he ran it over the flow line.

Pushing against stiff muscles, he shifted in the hide-covered chair and glanced at his jarl, Grenjad Thorfinn, on the nearby raised platform. The same place he'd been sitting for the past two hours, playing chess in the opening phase of negotiations with Ornolf Bjornssen, chieftain of the adjoining region. All this for the right to fish a particular stretch of the Hvítá River.

Waiting never sat well with Enar, and his muscles rebelled against being confined in this meeting room with the rest of the soldiers at Thorfinn's disposal. All he could hope was that a compromise could be reached soon, or the matter would go before the Althing in the summer. If that occurred, he'd be subjected to two more weeks of meetings and discussions. An event that would only prove worthy if he enjoyed the company of a beautiful and lusty woman.

So far, the only women he'd seen had made a single pass through the hall, delivering the meal. Most likely thralls too easily coaxed to a man's bedroll for a coin or two. Not to his liking. Enar's curiosity still burned over the rumor of the chieftain's sisters, who were professed to be great beauties.

A shout went up and the men sitting at the table on the raised platform shook hands.

Jarl Bjornssen scanned the room and lifted a beckoning hand. "Bring in more mead. We'll have another game."

"What a half-troll," Enar muttered, and jammed his elbows on the table.

"Quiet, my friend," a hushed whisper sounded. "Thorfinn will have your balls if your hotheadedness disrupts these talks."

"You know as well as I that a champion from each clan should be designated. Then let the duo battle with the victor claiming fishing rights for his clan."

"And you'd be the one chosen?"

His chin jerked in a sharp nod. "I am the best warrior in battle."

"Only in battle?"

Enar glanced at his closest friend, Bekan Crosby, and recognized the mirth in his battle-mate's green eyes. "Come to the arena and match swords. My muscles twitch from idleness."

Footfalls sounded in the rushes on the floor. A thrall, dressed in a typical coarse linen shift, stood at the end of the table holding a metal pitcher in both hands.

"Have you known me to pass on mead?" Bekan glanced at the dark-haired woman and gave her a wide smile. He grabbed his drinking horn and lifted it.

Stifling a groan at his friend's obvious lust, Enar shoved back his chair and stood. He tucked the tusk into a loop at the back of his belt and returned the knife to its sheath. With hands clasped in front of his body and his chin lowered in deference, he waited for Thorfinn's notice before exiting the long house. A formality that rankled his freeman's soul.

At his jarl's nod, Enar spun and strode through the carved wooden doorway and into the cool night. He sucked in deep breaths, glad for clear air that didn't smart his eyes almost to tears. If the decision was to be made by the sword, he vowed to be ready.

From the edge of the boulder, Jorunn Bjornsdatter watched a soldier from Thorfinn's clan practicing with a long sword on a suspended hay-stuffed bag. Only twenty paces separated them, so she hugged the rock to avoid detection. Sweat beaded on his bulging muscles and glistened in the moonlight. With each jab and swing, the man uttered a guttural moan. "Hah." A wooden shield ringed with metal chopped at the bag. "Huh."

A shiver ran through her at the sight of the warrior's bare chest, accented with bold runic tattoos. Her fingers itched to run over his golden skin, to test the solidity of his taut flesh.

Long enough had she sat in the women's circle, tending her sewing or weaving, and listening to the married women talk of the excitement lurking between a man's legs. The exertion displayed before Jorunn was vigorous and savage, and in the past she'd turned away from such sights. But tonight she felt spell-cast, unable to drag her gaze from the enchanting rhythm of his skilled moves.

This warrior with the wheat-colored braid running down the center of his scalp captured her attention. Tingles ran over her skin, centering in her breasts and making them plump. Not even a chill breeze to blame for her tits tightening into buds that poked against her flax-linen dress. A flush infused her cheeks and she palmed her breasts, pressing hard in hopes of easing the tension. But her touch only thrummed her blood faster, and Jorunn couldn't resist a squeeze or two, dragging her fingers along the fine cloth and twisting the tight nibs. Jolts of pleasure sparked in her lady flower, and she squeezed her thighs together, biting down on her lower lip to keep silent. Her head dropped backward, and she gazed at the pinpoints of starlight as she fought to catch her breath, pressing her heated body against the cool rock.

When her fiery passion ebbed and she felt in control again, she leaned to the side to watch the soldier. The arena was empty. She gasped and scanned the area, her shoulders drooping at the lost chance to meet a man from outside her clan. All her clansmen—she still thought of them as mere boys—kept separate for fear of offending their jarl. She'd never asked to be a descendant of Arnarson, the First Settler, or the sister of their chieftain.

Both hands balled into fists, and she swallowed back a scream of frustration. With jerky steps, she wended through the copse of birch trees and headed to the mineral baths. Might as well enjoy a hot bath. When her absence was discovered, she would have to suffer yet another lecture from her older sister Thorunn on the importance of protecting her virtue. A steamy soak would be her reward tonight...as small as it was.

Through the trees, silvery wisps of steam danced over the blue-green pool lined with stones. The strong scent of minerals reached her, and she wrinkled her nose. The soothing waters' single disadvantage. After emerging from the trees, she stepped onto the ring of flat stones surrounding the pool and moved toward a stone bench. Above it stretched a carved wooden arch with the rune *othala*. The diamond supported by two angled braces proclaimed this land as their spiritual birthright.

With deft fingers, she untied the bindings on her sandals, unclasped the chain at her waist, and then reached for the brooch holding her gown at the shoulder.

A clunk of metal against wood sounded.

Jorunn whirled and stared at the sauna hut ten feet past the steaming pool. Her lips mouthed a prayer. *Frigg, watch over me. Mother Goddess, keep me safe.* Whoever enjoyed the sauna had more right to be here than she did. Indecision froze her muscles.

"Rahhh." The hut door opened and out dashed the naked warrior.

Too shocked to make a sound, Jorunn could only gape as the soldier strode across the stones. Her gaze took in the loose-limbed walk accompanied by swinging arms that made his erect shaft bob in counteraction. Dryness attacked her throat and she swallowed hard. His manhood looked very much like excitement...if only the man had the ability to speak in more than single syllables.

The man eased into the pool and then stroked across its length, his sturdy arms chopping through the water. He flipped and turned at the far edge and then surfaced and extended a stiff arm her way. "You."

Panic invaded her chest and blood roared in her ears. The stranger had spied her. "I will leave you." She grabbed her sandals and turned toward the forest.

"Are you not trained to serve visitors?"

With great trepidation, she looked over her shoulder.

The warrior stood in the middle of the pool, water lapping at an abdomen knotted with taut muscles. Standing with hands fisted on his hips, his hair kept off his face by a silver circlet and its length streaming over one shoulder, he looked like Thor, god of thunder. A sound she would definitely hear if this guest mentioned her wanton behavior to her brother.

The challenge in his narrowed gaze raised her chin and squared her shoulders. She straightened and turned to face him, judging the distance between them to be enough for her to escape if she must. Except her shoes were still clutched in her hands. "I am." She opened her hand and the sandals dropped with a clump to the stones. Using her most graceful steps, she walked to the edge of the pool and dipped into a short bow, palms touching in front of her chest. Why wasn't any of her family around to see how well she accomplished these moves? Keeping her chin tucked, she watched him with sideways glances.

"I am in need of a cloth for drying." His gaze ran up and down the length of her shift dress.

The very shift she had intended to use to dry herself. Oh, why hadn't this meeting occurred in winter when she could offer her overskirt? She resisted rolling her eyes, remembering

Thorunn's reprimand that the action gave her the appearance of a maiden younger than her twenty years. "All I have is my dress." Two fingers pinched the cloth at her thigh and she pulled it out, making the fabric cling to the curves of her other side.

"Mmm, I see." He shifted in the pool and appraised her body with a bold stare. "That will have to suffice."

"Sir, I—" What could he mean? Her head jerked up and she met his gaze. Certainly not that she… Her tits tightened and pointed through her shift.

He strode closer and held up a staying hand. "Enar…not Sir."

"Enar." She acknowledged his name and waited as he approached the edge. Maybe he'd desist if he knew her rank. "My name is Jorunn."

His stare didn't flicker, and his movements didn't falter. His arms bunched so he could propel his body from the pool. Then he stood on the flat stones, steamy water swirling from his skin, twisting as it moved over the hills and valleys of his form, and pooling at his broad feet. "Commence, if you will."

Jorunn's heart pounded, and she dragged her gaze from his cock that erupted from the curly brown hair at his groin. "You want me to dry you?" She couldn't prevent the squeak at the end of her question. Underneath the mineral smell of the waters, she detected an earthy man scent that pleased her. But to touch him…

Freya, be praised. Her fingers fumbled as she unclasped the brooch from the folds of her garment, and then squatted to place it on a nearby stone. Bunching the fabric in her hands, she stood, bundle clutched at her chest. Naked as a babe, her only covering were the silver bangles wrapping her upper arms. Her skin heated and she knew her cheeks flamed like the red poppies covering the headlands. In a small way, she hoped her form pleased this warrior named Enar.

She sucked in a deep breath and moved around his side to dab the cloth across his broad shoulders, stretching on tiptoes to dry his neck. Long ridges of scars marred his wide back. Imagining the pain they'd caused him made her stomach flip.

"Are you aware, Jorunn, that spying from the shadows is not the best display of manners?"

He'd known she was there? For a moment, her hand stilled and then swiped down the bow of his spine. "I do not think spying is the correct word, s—uh, Enar."

His body shifted, and he looked over his shoulder, brows lowered over tawny eyes, transforming his face into a hawk-like expression. "What word is correct?"

She bit back a gasp and jerked up her chin. "Admiration. I was watching your style, admiring your parry and thrust." *There, she'd deflected that well.*

Enar snorted and turned all the way around, holding his arms out straight from his body. "My parry and thrust?"

Keeping her gaze locked with his, she pressed the bundled cloth along the top of one arm. "Exactly."

"Watching my...style involves pleasuring your sweet mounds tipped as pink as unripe cloudberries?" A brown eyebrow arched, but the edges of his eyes crinkled.

"Oh, Hela's blood. You saw that?"

He leaned close, his large hands cupping her shoulders. "That is why I hightailed for the sauna."

She gasped and her eyes shot wide.

"I'd hoped to steam away my fuc—" His gaze narrowed and he cleared his throat. "Um, my urges."

Surely, tomorrow she wouldn't show her face to a single

soul...especially this man. But tonight, the evening breeze tickled her skin, the stars sparkled in an inky sky, and she'd been given this unique chance to speak of such matters. Holding her breath tight in her chest, she dared lower her gaze to his golden chest and the black symbols marking the mounded flesh above his brown nipples. With a shaky hand, she reached to touch his skin, delighted by the warmth under her fingertips.

"Jorunn, you should not—"

"No proclamations. I hear enough from my family." She let the cloth fall to her feet and stepped close enough to feel the rounded head of his cock against her belly. Shiver bumps covered her skin. "Enar from the clan Thorfinn, I wish to be kissed. Will you grant me that wish?"

"Kissed? Wish?" His hands released her shoulders and he stepped back...falling into the steaming water.

Her gaze narrowed. She'd been so close. He must not escape. Jorunn followed him into the water, relishing the delicious sensation of tiny mineral bubbles moving over her body. She stroked after his retreating form, putting to use her many hours of ocean practice. On the eighth stroke, her hand wrapped around a solid calf covered in bristly hair. With sheer determination, she held tight.

They surfaced, her chest against his rigid side, water streaming over their faces. Enar braced himself, fighting against the natural male instinct that pounded through his veins. Seize and conquer.

He'd been a fool to tease like he had. But until Jorunn's fingers fumbled with the brooch on her dress, he hadn't known the extent of her innocence. The beautiful, blue-eyed maiden hadn't realized the double meaning of her reason for watching him. Parry and thrust. He knew exactly where he wanted to thrust his—

"Does my face or shape disgust you? Or maybe you are put off by my smart tongue." She blinked, but water clung to her lashes like silver dust. "I have been—"

With a muffled groan, he lifted a finger and pressed it against her lips to gain a moment of silence to order his thoughts. Whoever had planted the idea of Jorunn's appearance being disgusting should be gutted with a rusty blade. The warm body in his arms belonged to a young woman who was of age but remained untouched. A virgin...in his arms. Unable to control himself, his prick surged, and he twisted his hips to the side.

Sucking in a huge breath, he tipped back his head and sought the comfort of the everlasting nightly stars. Familiar sights he'd seen during many a raiding march. Not only was she untouched, but never kissed. That meant she must be part of the ruling family. He jerked and whipped his head downward to stare into her beseeching gaze, setting her at arm's length. "You're one of the sisters. Your brother is chieftain."

"That's not my fault." Her lips pressed into a tight line.

Under the surface, a warm toe traced a circle on his knee and moved up his thigh. "Stop doing that."

"You don't like my foot massage?"

Her questing toe advanced toward his hip. "Jorunn." Enar forced sternness into his tone when all he wanted was for her foot to move a bit toward the center, toward his aching cock. His fingers tightened and his jaw clenched.

"One stupid kiss is all I want. Why can't you—?" Her body stilled and her eyes popped wide. "Oh, perhaps your injuries have, um, reduced your ardor?"

The slam on his manhood cracked his resolve. His gaze became a steely stare. "Reduced...my...ardor?" The three words rasped through stiff lips.

60

Jorunn's words cut off, and her mouth gaped like a landed haddock.

How was he to gain lasting glory in this lifetime if his virility was questioned? Odin's teeth, the woman drove him mad. He stepped wide, seeking comfortable perches upon which to brace his feet, and relaxed his arms.

The change in tension floated her body closer and he ran a hand over her smooth shoulder, feeling every curve and hollow. Her flesh was firm, like her activity of choice was not sitting in the long house's communal room and stitching. *Go slow, she's untouched.*

His thoughts warred with the lust raging through his body. Too many weeks spent on raids and marches kept him from the comely wenches in Thorfinn's village. For just a moment, he touched his forehead to hers, murmuring sweetlings to remind him of her inexperience. "Breathe with me, *meyla*."

Her head jerked back. "I'm not a young girl, I'm a woman." She grabbed his hand from her shoulder and planted it on a high breast.

Enar snarled an unmentionable epithet and ordered his hand not to move, not to feel her nipple bud against his palm, not to heft its pert weight. Gritting his teeth, he growled a single word. "Breathe." He inhaled through his nose, drawing in the faint aroma of violets from her flaxen hair.

Jorunn followed his example, the inhalation pressing her breast tighter against his grasp.

Through three more commingled breaths, Enar thought of how to get himself out of this situation. Logic told him a short kiss would cause no harm. They couldn't go further because look where they were—surrounded by steamy water, hard rocks and dark forest. No place to consummate—

Thor's hammer, what was he thinking? No consummation, just a friendly kiss. Maybe he'd coax a little response so she'd know how to handle her next one. At that thought, his hand tightened, molding her soft breast.

Jorunn sighed and a hand rested on his chest, fingers outlining his tattoos and rubbing dangerously close to—

Zing. Her finger grazed his tight bud. A stern voice sounded in his head that he risked his place in Valhalla for what he was about to do. But in her presence, he was helpless. The act was foretold the moment he saw her face avid with curiosity peeking around the rock. Without another thought to the repercussions, he slanted his head and covered her mouth with his closed lips.

Teacher to student, he intended to apply the right amount of solid pressure for the appropriate interval. Maybe even change angles. He lifted his head and watched her lips form into a pout as she leaned forward. With an arm around her shoulders, he pulled her close, fighting hard to ignore the sweet press of her thatch on his throbbing cock. He kissed her again, molding his lips over hers, tasting her sweetness, relishing her eager response.

When her hand delved into his braid and held tight, he changed tactics. The woman kissing him, eating at his lips, entwining her leg with his, was not as innocent as she'd proclaimed. Enar eased his mouth back so his tongue could trace the rim of her mouth. His hands roamed her back and cupped her ass, lifting her to straddle his thigh. The water helped but she seemed to weigh less than the arsenal he wore and carried into battle.

At his move, Jorunn broke the exciting kiss and raised heavy eyelids. "What are you doing?"

"Shh." A calloused finger traced over her wrinkled brow,

along her temple and down her jaw. "You got a kiss. In truth, there were two kisses. Are you happy?"

His touch made her want. She needed his touch on other parts of her body—her budded nipples, the tender skin at the sides of her breasts, and on the pulsing knot between her thighs. "I have my kisses but I am not happy. I ache and itch all over." She wiggled her shoulders, hoping the increased flow of water would soothe her inflamed skin.

Enar grumbled beneath his breath and his hands settled on her hips. "Would you like the ache to go away?"

His fierce stare scared her a little but she refused to bow to the challenging glint she saw in his hazel eyes. "Yes, and I'd like to taste your tongue."

With a shake of his head, he chuckled. "You possess more knowledge than most untouched innocents."

"For years, I've placed my chair behind the loom at the women's circle." She canted her head and looked out from the sides of her eyes. "I'm a good listener and remember well."

As a smile pulled at the corner of his mouth, Enar eased her straddled thighs along his, pushed her back and pulled her forward again.

The rub of her tender knot against his bristly hair and taut muscle swirled yearning through her body. She braced her hands on his forearms and arched her back, stretching for the sweet release that only her own fingers had ever produced. His warm mouth covered her left nipple and he suckled, easy at first and then with strong tugs that echoed the rhythm of her lady flower sliding on his thigh. Sensations crashed through and over her body and she climaxed. A strangled cry wrenched from her throat, and her breath panted out in short huffs.

Enar released her nipple and pressed kisses over her skin,

over the curve of her breasts and up to the sensitive hollow at the base of her neck, nibbled kisses that ran along the column of her neck. A strong hand grabbed a hank of her hair and held her immobile as his mouth covered hers.

His tongue pushed between her lips and plundered the inside of her mouth, coaxing her tongue to join the exploration of warm lips, slick teeth and hard palates. This was *the* kiss. Her heartbeat sounded in her ears, and she snuggled closer to taste more, her hands roving over the hardness of his body. Not close enough. She bent her right leg and angled her toes along the inside of his thigh.

The rasp of an indrawn breath sounded and he sucked harder on her tongue, a hand clasped her breast.

Jorunn walked her toes over the crest of his thigh and centered her pulsing twatchel against his rigid spear. If she flexed her hips and pressed just right—

With a muffled roar, Enar scooped up her body and rose from the water like Thor marching from a stormy sea. Taking long strides, he carried her across the stones and laid her on the bench under the carved arch. His hands ran along her legs and pressed them open.

Her muscles were shaky, and she trembled, as weak as a newborn lamb. She crooked one knee and let the other leg hang over the bench's edge, not caring about her immodest posture.

Enar kneeled at her side, running a hand along her thighs, his gaze taking in her body that glowed in the silvery moonlight. Then his head dipped.

So, this was love's most intimate kiss. She sucked in a breath and felt warm air on her tingling knot a moment before his mouth devoured it. The tip of his tongue circled the nub and plunged along her woman's petals, setting her nerves afire.

Never before had she felt pulses so deep in her womb, or had the knot tightened as hard. Vaguely, she was aware Enar stroked his shaft and his mouth tugged harder. After only a finger-tweak or two on her nipples, she felt the wave of excitement engulf her senses.

This time, she lifted her head and connected with Enar's gaze. As brazen as a sex thrall. Wanting him to see the effect his touch created on her body. When her arms trembled, she lay back and luxuriated in his soft caresses on her body. Moments stretched and he sat beside the bench, his head cradled in her lap. She ran her fingers along his thick braid, and smoothed them over the shaved scalp around his ears.

Only moments or maybe a lifetime later, Enar stood at her side, fully dressed. He leaned over to lace up her sandals and ease her damp shift over her body, securing the brooch and snapping the chain belt.

As she stood, she brushed kisses along his stubbled jaw. "I thank you for granting my wish."

A grin pulled at the side of his mouth. "My pleasure, Jorunn."

Their walk through the forest was silent, but filled with subtle touches and caresses. At the edge of the village, Jorunn whispered, "Better not walk farther together."

Enar squeezed her hand and brushed a lingering kiss on her cheek.

With slow and tiny steps, she walked toward her family's corner of the long house, her gaze following Enar's long strides as he moved toward the circle of cloth tents. When he disappeared inside one, she followed, silently asking Freya's blessings. Jorunn lifted the flap and moonlight slid across Enar's broad chest and naked legs. Her mouth dried.

A frown creased his brow and he pushed up on one elbow. "Are you all right?"

For a moment, her breath caught in her throat. Before her was a magnificent warrior who had just treated her as gently as a kitten. A man she wanted and needed at her side. She nibbled on her lower lip. "I have another wish."

Grinning, Enar lay back and opened his arms wide. "Come and tell me, my sweet."

My Loveliest Vision

Renee Luke

Lion's Castle, England, 1192 AD

She was no longer alone.

Ignoring the man who had invaded the privacy of her small herb garden, Lena of Lion's Castle buried her hands into the soil, found a clod of dirt and broke it up with her fingers. The pungency of the earth, the sweet freshness of thyme, the dewiness of morning did nothing to veil the masculine smell of musk, leather and sandalwood. His scent lingered on the soft zephyr, teasing and taunting the aromas of spring.

Feeling the sharpness of his stare as a prickle down her spine, Lena slanted her face to the sky, bathing her skin in the glorious warmth of the sun, sensing the man behind her as she did dawn after a long, dark night.

He was not the first nor would he be the last to infest her keep, to attempt to claim her, to occupy these holdings by force if need be. Nay, the untimely death of her father and the lack of a male heir lured the vilest of lechers, the most loathsome, despicable men.

At least this one bathes, she thought, catching the hint of lye as she inhaled the tepid air kissed by the early rays of the day.

Beneath her knees the ground trembled with his footfall as the man moved a step closer. His massive presence shrunk the stillness of her garden, destroying her serenity.

Fear coiled low in her belly. Swiping a frolicking curl away from her face, she tucked the strand of hair behind her ear, swallowing down the terror as it blossomed. A fortnight had passed since the last devious knight had attempted seizure of her home and body, as if by arrival alone he had some sort of entitlement.

Her father's men had dealt with him swiftly, but few of them remained now, her protection quickly waning. Even lifelong servants deserted her, finding work where there was coin to be made. Surrounded by her life of darkness, Lena closed her eyes and listened to the man's breathing, the creaking of his leather boots as he shifted and the smooth, threatening glide of steel sliding in its scabbard.

She'd not face him as a coward. Gulping a deep breath, Lena rubbed her palms across her skirt, swiping away the dirt and dampness of fear. To her right, she wrapped her fingers around the well-worn handle of the wooden cane her father had carved for her and rose to her feet.

Lifting her chin and pulling back her shoulders, Lena turned and faced the man who lingered against the stone wall off the kitchens, near the creeping ivy where the rattling of leaves announced each of his movements.

"You should return to your home, milord," Lena said boldly, repressing the tremble in her voice, holding firmly to her cane lest her hands shake, ready to strike if he advanced upon her. "There's naught for you here."

She was greeted by silence. Tapping her toe to the ground once, identifying the worn garden path before stepping forward, Lena moved toward him, willing him to answer, to argue, to state his demands. The moment stretched, tension pounding behind her temples. His lack of response whittled away the fright and fashioned the drumming of her heart into annoyance.

"Have you no tongue, milord? No manners?"

She took a step closer, bridging the gap between them only slightly. The leaves rattled, then settled as the man remained quiet, but she could hear him breathing, could almost feel the warmth of his breath drifting in her direction.

"If you have not a word say, you have no business here." She lifted her cane and pointed it to her left, aiming it toward the garden gate. "Go!"

"I will not."

His voice was low. Rough. Determined. And there was something in his tone that teased her senses like a pastry long since tasted teased her palate. Had she heard his voice before or was it panic playing tricks with her memories? She wasn't sure, but he had spoken only three words. However, Lena knew to her core she was in trouble. Fear took hold again, edging away the bits of annoyance as she rifled her memories, trying to summon one that matched his voice.

She remained steady, facing forward to where the man stood, fighting the gnawing trepidation and the need to call out for the few remaining of her father's men. They'd not get to her in time, she knew, if this man, this invader, sought to do her harm. She'd be dead by his hand before help would arrive.

"If you shall not leave, state your purpose here. My father

cannot be disturbed at the moment." Lena squeezed her lids closed, feeling the burn of tears. Tears she could not allow to fall. She pushed down the tightness in her throat. This man was different, his presence in her garden more of an incursion than any before. Her voice broke as she opened her eyes. "Milord, there is naught for you here."

"Your father is dead. And, you..."

The leaves rattled, and the earth trembled beneath her feet. "You are mine."

In a heartbeat he was upon her. Overpowering in presence as the air was crushed between them. She fought the need to step back, to gain distance from this intruder. But it was too late. He was large, she could tell by how his shoulders blocked the warmth of the sun, replaced instead by his heat and the heady scent of man: leather, lye, sweat and sunshine. And again, of exotic sandalwood.

Strong fingers embraced her wrist. She startled at his touch, sucking in a gasp between her lips. His touch was warm, calloused, but so unexpectedly gentle she didn't pull away. For a moment fear was overrun by the enthralling heat of him. The intoxicating male scent. She stood allowing him to touch her skin. Almost enjoying the way it made heat spread through her.

"Lena..."

He cleared his throat, stepping closer, and her hand brushed against the material of his tunic. He was firm beneath, flesh forged of steel. Heat increased as it flowed through her.

His breath danced below her ear. "Milady, I shall not force myself upon you, but know this; you are already mine for the taking."

Reality crushed her, and trepidation followed fear down her spine. She twisted her hand attempting to free herself from his hold and yet hesitated to sever the contact. His grasp was unbreakable. "My father will not stand..."

"Lena, your father is dead," he said, his voice soft but firm, "and had he not been, he'd still not halt my claim of you." He released his hold on her.

She could hear the sound of worn leather as he fumbled with his belt. And then he was touching her again, taking her hand in his. With her palm up, he first ran the rough pad of his thumb across her flesh, causing her to quiver, then replaced his thumb with a scroll of parchment.

Lena turned her face to the sky while she steadied her breathing. Attempted to slow her fitful pulse. Her stomach churned with fear and something unfamiliar that pooled dew upon her tender lips and caused her inner thighs to go slick.

The parchment meant something. Biting down on her tongue, she remained silent, already resigned. Closing her eyes, she lowered her face. "You have no claim to my holdings," she said, her voice less firm than it had been before. "No claim to me."

He chuckled. "You are wrong, milady, but you needn't believe my words." He curled the hand which held hers, forcing her fingers to tighten around the scroll. "You may read the truth in your father's words."

She shrugged free of his hold, then spun away so her back absorbed his heat. *Could it be...?* She dropped her cane and touched both hands to the scroll, finding the wax seal with her fingertips. *Could it be?* Memories came rushing upon her all at once. "Seth..." she whispered, carefully tracing her father's signet ring that had so long ago been pressed into the wax.

"'Tis I, milady."

He spoke, but the sound echoed in her ears as memories

commanded her attention. The garden walls melted away. As did the years, the past tucked away in shadows.

Her father gave her hand away. She'd heard their voices, their agreements and arrangements, the rustling of the parchment, the screech of his quill and the shift of earth as she slid down the wall to the floor.

Lena struggled with the lump in her throat and the confusing yearning that caused a heaviness in her breasts. She held the scroll to her chest as she considered her fate. A fate she'd set aside as so many moons had passed.

She turned toward him. "So you are to be my husband." She began to tremble, her emotions clawing free. "Milord...Seth." A drop escaped the corner of her eye, so she bent down and felt along the bed of garden herbs for her cane, to keep him from seeing the tears betraying her.

Seth watched her intently, expecting her to fight him, or flee, but she did neither. She bent, one hand fumbling through weeds on the ground as she attempted to veil a sob. And he'd not missed the tear sliding down her creamy skin as she stooped to find her cane.

Her cane? Aye, he knew now what was different about her, why she seemed unaffected by him when other women swooned. Why she seemed to look through him or past him, but never into his eyes.

She was blind.

Anger coiled in his belly. At her father for not sending for him as soon he'd first fallen ill. He'd left his daughter unprotected. This beautiful girl with raven hair and green eyes as silvery as sage, with lips that appeared stained by rose petals and flawless skin. He could well imagine the hateful lechers and vermin she'd been left to handle on her own. It would be hard enough for any lady, harder still for one that could not see.

Another emotion crept in, something more aligned with affection and fiercely protective. He'd never allow this woman who'd bravely faced him to be harmed. Not by anyone else, and surely not by him.

Though desire had turned his cock to stone the very moment he'd first touched her, he'd be faithful to his word. Although they were betrothed, as good as wed, he'd not force himself upon her. Instead, he'd imperceptibly persuade her to seduce him.

Aye, the convincing would commence now. He stooped and retrieved her cane from the ground, then gently placed it in her free hand, but did not release his own hold. As she gripped the worn, whittled wood, he moved it toward him so she'd be forced to step closer or let go.

She was molded perfectly to his taste, swollen breasts pressed against her bodice revealing shadows one day—soon—he'd explore. With fingers and then his tongue. Seth nearly laughed when he heard her catch her breath, but the feisty wench didn't move away.

She'd plaited her hair, but twisting curls escaped. One day, he'd catch those curls in his grasp as he held her steady to the bed and worked his cock between her thighs. Lust heated his blood, soothing away the last remnants of his anger. He touched her cheek, not surprised when she went motionless at the contact.

"Milord?"

"You've soil upon your skin." Once the dirt was brushed away, Seth continued touching her, his fingertips lingering, then slowly trailing down silken skin to the pulse beating in her neck.

She trembled, but instead of leaning away, she pressed closer. An invitation.

Bending, he touched his mouth to where his fingers had been. He licked, then chuckled against her when her heartbeat responded eagerly to him. He cupped a hand beneath one breast, testing the weight in his palm. When she sucked a breath, he moved his mouth to her lips and staked his claim. Aye, she tasted as sweet as the rose petal lips would smell, feminine and honeyed. And though caught by surprise, she didn't move away. She arched into him, filling his hand and offering her mouth for the taking.

A moan mingled on their shared breath, hers soft and tempting. Bold, as he'd known this brave waif would be, she touched her tongue to his, then followed his lead.

She was his. She already belonged to him, and as such, he had the right to take her where and when he pleased. Need mingled with reason as he fought back the urge to lay her down upon the garden beds and push her skirts to her tiny waist, ease her legs apart and have a taste of lips he was sure were wet and waiting for him. Aye, he'd fuck her until she cried out his name, fuck her until she shook with release, fuck her until he came.

But he'd made an oath to not force her. Seth broke the kiss and stepped away, a hand remaining upon Lena's arm to steady her when she swayed. He was breathing hard, his cock heavy and demanding, in revolt as it throbbed against his leggings.

There was a shimmer in the silvery green of her eyes as she lifted her chin and pulled back her shoulders. Not tears this time, but defiance. And desire.

"You are to be my husband," she said steadily.

He knew the words were meant to justify her willingness to be kissed.

She soothed her tongue across the plump flesh as if getting another taste. "Aye, my husband. But, milord," she lifted the parchment toward him, "you have known of this. You came here to claim my holdings. Me. Whereas, I..." She paused and inhaled, her body shuddering. Doubt and apprehension resurfaced upon her face. "I haven't thought of my betrothal for years."

Seth bent and brushed her lips one more time, a quick caress, not liking the fear shining in her eyes when what he wanted was the mirroring of his arousal and the awakening of her need. "Aye, milady, you belong to me, but instead of claiming you, I shall make you beg." To keep from making himself a liar, he turned and walked away.

Lena paced before Seth's chamber, waiting for him to retire for the night. The sun had come and gone a score of times, and in all those days, they'd only shared quick exchanges. He teased her with his presence here, making it known he was in full control—of her father's men, the hall, but also her.

Each morning when she'd left her room, his scent, musky and masculine, enticed her into the hall. When they broke their fast, he couldn't keep his hands from her—on her arm to help her find her seat, her thigh when they sat close, her face in the guise of brushing away a crumb or two, and her lips with soft kisses for each of their greetings and farewells.

Aye, he was controlling her by demanding every thought, for whether he was nearby or not, he remained imbedded firmly in her mind.

Pausing, Lena exhaled a shaky breath. And it wasn't just her waking hours that were consumed with thoughts of her betrothed, but every dream, every night. When she lay in bed, thoughts of him manifested into sultry dreams that roused her from sleep with her clitoris throbbing and her nipples beaded tightly. The nightly torment coupled with all his casual touches had unleashed a liquid heat into her blood. His casual kisses held her on the edge of begging for deeper, more intimate kisses.

Aye, he'd commanded control of her by making no demands at all.

Lena drew in a long breath and clamped her thighs together to ward off the throbbing between her legs. Tapping her cane along the stone wall, she located his door, then moved to stand in front of it. Unaccustomed to being manipulated, she planned on turning the tables on him. "Nay, milord, it will be *you* who begs," she whispered, eager now to wait inside for Seth's return.

"I shall beg for what, milady?"

Lena gasped. So deep in thought, she'd missed the spicy scent and slight vibrations on the stone floor announcing his arrival. "Beg, milord? Nay, I merely said…" Her voice trailed off when he began to chuckle. Lifting her chin, she collected her fleeting courage. "Seth, you are to be my husband, but I have yet to see you."

Silence greeted her for a moment, but she felt the heat of him as he stepped closer. Felt the caress of his breath feather along her skin when he whispered, "Nay, milady, you have not. But as you are mine, I am likewise yours. You are free to touch if you so desire."

Lena didn't wait. Lifting a hand, she touched his cheek and was greeted by a roughness that hadn't seen a blade in several days. The prickle awakened her senses. Her folds grew wet. Her sex throbbed in time with her heartbeat. Feeling emboldened by her yearning, she moved across his cheek to trace the curve of his lips. A breath curled around her fingertips. Dropping her cane, she lifted a second hand to his face and traced the line of his jaw, the shape of his nose, the arch of his brow above his eyes, creating an image of him.

He was beautiful in his power, all straight lines and strength, with lips that knew how to kiss. Lifting on tiptoes, she reached for him, touching his mouth with her own, then running her tongue across his lower lip.

"You've had mead, milord." She ran her tongue across his, then nibbled his bottom lip, nipping lightly with her teeth. Lena left his mouth, smoothing her tongue along his skin, as she trailed down his neck to his pulse.

"Aye." Seth clamped his jaw tight, fighting the desire to snatch her up. When had this virgin waif turned into a temptress? A seductress? A siren? *Hell's breath*, her delicate hands clung to his tunic, her mouth teased him, her scent was sweetened with roses. With arousal.

Desire, raw and restless, clawed him, but he stayed his hand and allowed her to lead, a feat that tested him. "Is my face the only part you're curious to see, milady?"

"Milord?" she said, in a breathy whisper.

He berated himself for his impatience because she'd stopped her tantalizing assault. Her brows furrowed together as her silvery green eyes looked past him. And then she smiled, her pink lips wet, slightly swollen.

"Nay, milord." Her fingers found the leather ties of his leggings.

His cock, rock solid and heavy with lust, sprung into her hands. Her breathing changed, and her silver eyes shimmered with a need.

He growled as she curved her fingers around him, holding him softly at first, then tightening as she slid her soft hand to his base. When she retraced the length of him, a bead of arousal was drawn to his tip. She felt it, running a thumb across his head. Drawing out a slick series of circles.

Before he knew what she was about, Lena had dropped to her knees and replaced her thumb with lush lips and an eager tongue.

He groaned, the whisper of her name gravelly as it escaped, "*Lena.*"

"Let me look, Seth." Her lips moved against his flesh as she spoke, her breath dancing across his skin.

One hand settled beneath his sack, taking the weight in her palm. The other hand continued the slow reconnoitering strokes up and down his shaft. Her mouth opened around him, taking him into the balmy depths while her tongue teased along his ridge.

'Twas a woman's instinct she toiled with, naught more. With each caress she was emboldened, closing her fingers around him more tightly as she worked his cock with unhurried strokes.

Seth grasped her locks, the dark tresses winding like silken ties around his wrists. Holding her hair to the side, he looked down so he could watch. Watch her full lips work up and down his length. Watch enthralled when she licked the moisture from his tip, only to begin again. Arousal gathered at his base. As amazing, as mesmerizing as her mouth felt, nay, they were not the lips he longed to be encased inside.

Would her pussy be as wet, her lips as swollen, she so eager, if he pushed her to the wall and fucked her quim instead of her mouth? Aye, he'd find out. He eased from her mouth and lifted her from the floor.

Lena had been lost in his taste. Lost in the silk-over-steel feel of him. Lost in the sounds he made which proved control slipped away from him. And she was gaining it.

Until he pulled from her mouth, grabbed her around the waist and backed her against the cold stone wall of the hallway outside his chamber.

A determined hand dove beneath her skirts and behind a knee as he lifted her leg to drape over his forearm, opening her thighs, slick with desire for him.

His other hand brought the head of his cock to her moist lips. He rubbed between them, then pressed his hard rod to her nubbin until she shook, the unnamed need of her dreams now known as emptiness. Named lust.

"I made a promise."

He eased forward, perhaps an inch, not enough that she could feel herself stretch.

"I promised I would not force you, milady." His lips grazed her cheek, nipped her earlobe. "Lena, you must beg."

Lena shook her head. Betrothed or not, she'd not beg a man. She'd already lost so much, she'd not lose her will. "Nay, milord."

Reaching up, she entangled her fingers in his hair and dragged his face down. She pressed her lips to his, heat uncurling when his tongue touched hers. With the other hand, Lena reached between their bodies and closed her fingers around his metal-forged cock. Taking the lead, she eased him a little deeper between her folds, arching off the wall to make room for him.

She broke off the kiss. "Nay, Seth. You beg."

He laughed. A husky sound of pleasure that made her smile. "I thought my wife to be a lady, but you're a vixen." He kissed quick and firm on her mouth.

Lena knew one sharp thrust of his hips and he'd be encased

inside her and there'd be nothing she could do to stop him. But he kept his word. Now, she intended to keep hers. "A vixen of your creation, milord." She eased him from between her slick lips. "Now, will you beg, or should I retire for the evening?"

He chuckled again, but the sound was tighter this time. His breathing more shallow. A sigh escaped. "I wanted you to beg me, dearest. So there would never be a question of your willingness. But you test me."

She bit her lip, holding still, afraid to speak because she knew the words would be a plea.

His body pressed harder into hers. "*Let me in, Lena,*" came his raw whisper. "Open up and allow me entry." He kissed the sensitive skin below her ear. Nibbled lightly on her earlobe. "Please," he whispered. "Please."

Lena smiled at her triumph while moving his cock back within her pussy until he stretched her lips apart. "Claim what is yours, dear Seth."

And he did. Seth thrust into her, closing his mouth over hers to capture her cry when he broke through and sheathed himself to his base within her. He lifted her leg higher, attempting to make room within to ease whatever discomfort she might be feeling.

Seth groaned when she wiggled against him, her walls holding him tight, her silken fluid bathing his cock, dripping like honey to his balls. It took all of his willpower to remain still, to not slam into her again and again until he released the shower of arousal he'd been holding since the day in the garden.

But Lena did not remain still. She opened her mouth, allowing him to deepen the kiss, and began to move, using her leg over his arm as leverage. She began to ride the length of him, arching her back until only his head remained between her nether lips, then grinding back down until those same lips molded to his base.

Aye, his waif was a vixen, no doubt. A brave and demanding little thing. In this instant, she was demanding he come. He stood there intoxicated by her kiss while she rode him. She was tight around him. So wet. Her soft moans tasted like sugar on his tongue. Her moans turned into a scream as her body began to tremble and tighten around the length of his cock and liquid heat poured out.

And that was it. All he could take. A final thrust, and he poured into her, growling out his release as he came. When he was empty, when her breathing began to slow, when he could think again, he smoothed his lips across her skin to whisper in her ear, "Milady, do you like what you see?"

Lena of Lion's Castle, his betrothed wife, buried her face into the curve of his neck and laughed. "Aye, milord, you are my loveliest vision."

THE INVASION OF NEFYN

Lizzie Ashworth

Badon, Wiltshire, England, 496 AD

The latch on the heavy cottage door rattled, and my neck hair raised. I turned, thinking of the other villagers who, like me, had lingered. Were we caught off guard? No shouts of warning rang out. But the Saxons sometimes appeared from the forest like silent ghouls.

Another rattle, and the door yielded to his shoulder. His eyes, black as winter night, locked on me. His round shield bore the image of a red dragon and a longsword glinted in his fist.

I had waited, loath to remove the last of our belongings from the home of our family, where my children were born, where Bedwyr might return for a brief time and I could touch his face and know that he still lived. One more day, I promised myself, before I burdened the cow with bundles of bedclothes and meager portions of foodstuffs and drove her up into the mountains to join the others.

Luminous morning mist layered through the greening

valley, and against that brightness, his tall form loomed dark in the opening. Supple leather, marked with dents and scrapes of battle, clad his chest and loins. A baldric ornamented with gold medallions draped from his shoulder, a gold torque encircled his neck. Every inch of him bristled with menacing strength. After an instant frozen in his stare, I dropped the plunger into the half-churned butter and turned for my escape.

The whole of southern Britain bled. Whatever we did, they kept coming. By land, by sea, the horde of invaders drove west through the forests beyond the standing stones. Women, children, old and young died on their brutal axes. The bastards torched homes, stables screaming with livestock, whole villages.

Weary and scarred, our men stood to fight. They marched, fought, won, lost, fell back, regrouped, marched again. The rest of us fled before the invaders like hares before burning fields.

Clearly I had tempted fate too long. This morning, postponing my departure yet another day, I had set a fresh stew over the fire pit and turned to my tasks. Yet something of the day had already pricked my nerves, whether the heat of summer or the long quiet wait for news. A premonition, I knew now.

His sword and shield clattered to the rough boards of the table and in two steps, his hands seized me. My breath locked in my lungs. Gooseflesh raced up my arms as he pulled me back against him. Iron, muscled arms captured my waist and hips. In moments, he had torn away the cloak fastened at my shoulder and ripped open my linen robe, exposing my breasts to air.

"I mean to have you," he rasped at my ear. "In every way."

Shudders of trepidation plunged from my throat to my belly. I swallowed, unable to form words as his rough hands bruised over the sensitive skin. The flesh of my breasts burned under his touch and swelled against his palms.

"Mercy," I gasped.

"No mercy," he growled, yanking at the lower parts of my garments.

His fingers plowed into the thick hair between my thighs as I struggled.

"You may resist," he laughed, fingering me, "but a man is what you need."

His scarred fingers handled the moist crevice, pausing over the hardened pleasure knot. One big finger slid inside me.

"Oh!"

"Yes, sweet flower," he muttered. "Call for me."

The width of his hand spread my legs. His finger stroked inside me, pulling out the growing tide of juice, thumbing over the stiffened morsel so that I jerked and cried out. I lunged and twisted, fighting his arms. But I also weakened to his invasion.

With a growl, he shoved me forward over the table and lifted my skirt over my back. His hands grasped my buttocks. His thumbs dragged my cream as he pulled me open. I heard the shift of his clothing as his baldric fell aside, and then the hard knob of his cockhead probed between my legs.

He shoved inside me and drew in a sharp breath. Thick and long, his fleshy spear found its way deep into my belly. With my waist in the firm grip of his hands, I steeled myself to his plundering as he drew back for another thrust.

Our bodies shook in the force of his taking, both of us grunting and gasping with each shattering collision between his groin and my buttocks. His tensed sack swung against my engorged vulva in each forward lunge. The bristle of his bared legs chafed my inner thighs.

In that moment, I confess I wanted nothing more than to take him deep into my belly for as long as he would have me.

My heat rose, as did his own. Cock fire burned inside me. His coming raged along the shaft. Blasting in long hot surges, he called out with each lingering thrust.

I waited as he finished, my body gathered around the igneous mass he had delivered to my center. His clench at my waist lightened then strayed to again seize my breasts and slide along my sides to the front of my thighs. My quim pulsed, still holding him.

He stepped back, removing himself even though he remained erect. Hesitant, I turned.

"Nefyn," he whispered. His gaze seared over me before his lips crushed my mouth. "I've missed you."

I couldn't keep the tears away. They rolled from the corners of my eyes as I kissed him, as my hands combed through the tangles of sable hair that fell loose to his shoulders.

"Bedwyr, you torment me with your lovemaking." I laughed, joining his dark humor. "It gives me such happiness to see you." I pressed my face against his cheek, inhaling his scent. "Where is the enemy? How long can you stay?"

His thumbs brushed at my tears. He kissed me again, tenderly at first, but then his tongue probed mine, inciting us both.

"Only a short time," he replied. "In two days' march, we're to take our stand at Corinium. Arthur leads us, but King Meurig of Gwent faces his own threat and can't send men. And the Black Irish have crossed the Severn Sea and even now hold Kernow's western lands. We're greatly outnumbered." He thrust me back from him, frowning. "You were to be gone by now."

"Yes, I..."

His hands tightened, and his eyes narrowed. "Must I punish you?" His hands swept down the opened folds of my dress, thumbing my nipples until they hardened.

Flames licked over my skin. "My lord…"

"I don't know who harms me more," he grumbled in mock anger, "the enemy's sword or my wife's disobedience."

I barely heard his words. He licked and sucked at the rigid points. His calloused hands fondled and pulled the soft mounds of my breasts until I ached with need.

"Bedwyr," I begged.

His mouth curled in that familiar smile. He pulled me to his chest and kissed my hair. Such overpowering comfort in his arms—I wanted time to stop.

"Will you eat?" I asked finally.

"I have a fierce hunger, yes. But not yet for food."

On the stone hearth, the morning's fire lingered over a bed of glowing coals. I collected them under the stew pot and poured him a cup of water. We laughed together as he tugged me to the soft bedding at the corner of our cottage. His hands trembled as he took down the last of my garments, his gaze searing a path over my tumescent breasts and pebbled nipples, over the slight curve of my belly and thicket of dark hair. He reached toward me.

"No," I insisted, slipping around him. "Let me."

I released the fasteners of his tunic and skirt, setting the leather aside to tease my fingers over the linen undergarment. Each virile curve and bulge of his chest, shoulders, biceps and forearms garnered my rapt attention as I lifted the soft fabric over his head. Little space on his magnificent form escaped fading scars or dark red healing wounds. But that hardly marred his beauty. Robust and stalwart, his forearms and lower legs tanned, his abdomen white and carved with rock-hard ridges, he filled my vision as would a god.

I poured warmed water into a basin and bathed him,

removing dust, sweat and blood of battle. With the washing finished, my mouth trailed behind my fingers, eager to salve the worried skin. Only when he groaned did I relent in my greedy ministrations to focus my hunger at the apex of his legs. There his manhood stood ready, his stones drawn up tight.

"Tell me, my dear husband," I said, toying with the tip of my tongue. "You journeyed all this distance because you believed I'd be gone?"

"Headstrong but clever." He chuckled. "I'm reassured at how well I know you."

I licked the tender seam of his thigh and bristled sack, and chewed at the base of his thick cock. Veins laced over its darkening length. It pulsed against my lips, fever hot. His musky scent filled my nose, ripe with hints of horse and leather, woodland thickets, sharp spice. My mouth watered, so long deprived of his taste. My tongue spread over the column to curl from side to side on the long journey toward the exposed crown. Salty drops waited at its silken tip.

I sucked him in, past the gentle brush of my teeth, along the ridges on the roof of my mouth, deep to the back of my throat. My tongue pressed and massaged him, my cheeks tight in sucking. With each long delicious mouthful, my fingertips massaged his stones and the farther length of his prick, far below what I could fit into even the greatest reach of my throat. I needed him more than food or drink, this rich flavor, this thick miracle between my lips.

His heat rose, radiating off my face and swelling in my nose. I hovered over him, dragging my mouth up and down as his loins shuddered, demanding his gift as my long hair draped his abdomen. His hands clenched in the trailing lengths. He called on the gods and whispered my name.

The surge tightened first at my fingertips where his sack hardened. A rumbling cry rolled from his chest as his fire blazed up, discharging in thick torrents against the back of my tongue and into my throat. My nostrils flared with his taste—of salt, of chanterelles.

After a few moments, as I savored the last drops, his hands coaxed at my shoulders.

"Come here, my love."

He brought me to rest against his side. My leg draped possessively over his heavy thigh, my hand on the broad expanse of his chest. Gradually, our heartbeats slowed, and I wanted him always here under the touch of my hand. I would protect and warm him, feed him tender bread and rich meat, watch at the hilltop while he slept.

After a time, as the sun crested at midday, I roused against his protest to check the stew. The pot swung out on its hook over the fire and sent a savory aroma into the air as I stirred. Thick with leeks, turnips and carrots, the broth bubbled in lamb fat and thyme.

"It smells of sorcery," he laughed. "I've suffered for weeks on hard bread and salted fish."

"I like you to suffer. You appreciate me more," I replied, my eyebrow cocked.

Bedwyr rose and stalked toward me in his full naked glory, his loose hair partially covering his face. But his leer escaped that veil, warning as he pinioned me in his arms and made quick work of savaging me with his mouth. Nipples, buttocks and thighs peaked and shivered in the fast nips of his teeth. His lips grazed over my shoulders and down my spine. The tip of his tongue lingered at the crease of my buttocks, sending clenching bursts of desire through my bones.

"Put the lid on the stew pot, woman, before I drag you off."

Laughing, I obeyed his demand and was immediately lifted up and carried the short distance to our bed, where he stretched my arms above my head and used his other hand to torment the moist flesh between my legs. His face, full of pleasure and arrogant power, hovered over me, watching my response. I couldn't escape his knowing stare any more than I could escape the onslaught of his skilled manipulations, so that in only a short time I panted and writhed.

"Bedwyr, please."

A quiet chuckle rumbled in his throat. "Who suffers now?"

His leg captured the space between mine, nudging my thighs apart. Exquisite lances of joy shot through me as he held the rosebud and slid its fleshy hood up and down. When the strutted flesh drew the coils of my belly close to bursting, he deflected my impending eruption by stroking it coarsely with his thumb and then tracing his finger down between the slick folds to prod slightly into the opening of my vagina.

"Ohh, the gods!"

"Do you want me, wench?" he taunted.

"Yes, Bedwyr! Please!"

He inserted two fingers, shoving callously. My hips rose.

"My sweet flower," he whispered, curling over me to bring his mouth to the quaking flesh under his hand. He released my hands and brought both his arms under my hips, gripping my buttocks and forcing my knees into the air as he buried his face between my legs.

His tongue licked at the sensitive lips, jolting me with thrusts before returning to lap and suck at the throbbing sliver of nerves. His thumbs caressed the inner sides of my thighs. The broad rasp of his tongue swept over the width of my valley, piercing me in darting invasions and forceful strokes.

His fingers began a slow, deliberate rhythm inside me while his mouth focused on my quivering minge, now trembling on the edge of explosion. Heat gathered over my skin, bathing me in a film of sweat. My head tossed from side to side and I reached for him, urging, pleading.

"Not yet," he whispered. "Your nectar feeds me."

My cries only grew louder as the need in my belly grew. The rosebud swelled and hardened. My juices flowed over his hand. Still he plundered me, a finger now also probing my arse in the bath of fluid wetting us both.

The pyre ignited. Heat shot through my chest, spiraled through my belly and burned bright at the knot pulsing against his teeth before flaring inside with his hands. His fingers thrust fast and hard into my openings. I spasmed and grasped, turned and thrashed as my body seized in his ravishment.

In moments, he swept over me with the full force of his body, his rigid cock finding its path between my thighs. A new, more brittle craving consumed me as he pushed through my swollen folds. His length drove far inside, opening me to full surrender around his huge shaft. There, yes, he nudged the spot. Yes, there, he rocked against it, plowing me apart with each thundering surge.

My hands assailed his shoulders and back as he labored over me, grunting, sweat beading his chest and neck. His sack slapped between my buttocks. His hands gripped my shoulders. His mouth hovered over mine; his lips curled in that tantalizing smile. His eyes carried the message of his loins—need, caring, desire.

"I love you," he muttered between clenched teeth. "More than my life."

"I love you, too," I gasped. "And I love you in me, filling me with yourself."

He pumped in short thick strokes that buried him fully against me. Our breath came in gasps that matched the slickening sounds of our fucking. His body shook with the force of his control. Veins stood on his neck.

I felt it rising, this fire that raced through my muscle and centered around his fiery magic. Suddenly it seemed the stars of heaven cascaded through my forehead and scalp. My silken channel convulsed along his length. I felt him fight the sensation, give one last attempt to wait, but then with a cry, his seed flew out in a boiling torrent toward the mouth of my womb. His body arched with the offering of his loins, lifting my hips and bottoming against the bones of my pelvis.

We lay quietly in each other's arms, partly draped by the woolen blanket. I wanted him to rest, but each time I moved, his hands followed. Finally, I untangled my limbs and went to the hearth. He leaned up on an elbow to watch with half-lidded eyes.

"Will you eat now, wild man?"

"I might, witch, if you don't tempt me again."

With my hair pulled back in a tie, I slid into my loose linen shift to mix a quick batter for griddle bread. My satisfied smile grew each time I glanced over at him, his muscled shoulders gleaming in the room's light, his eyes never leaving me. When I squatted at the fireside and stirred the coals, he heaved himself up.

"What needs should I attend?" he asked, looking around. "Are you prepared to leave?"

He pulled his tunic over his body, distracting me with its hem that barely covered his taut buttocks.

"I only must roll up the bed and fasten all of it onto the cow."

"And what of the children?"

"Both of your young sons are healthy and already hard at work with my sister's flock, where she says they learn fast the ways of sheepherding. I've missed them." I watched him, my body soft and pliable as only he could make it. My mouth twisted in a wry smile. "If I were to guess, after today you'll have another child."

He kissed me, his arms locked so firmly around me I could hardly breathe.

"A daughter perhaps, as beautiful as her mother." He nestled his face against my neck, heating my skin, his hands warming my buttocks.

My heart contracted as I imagined him with our daughter, how he would laugh at her play and hover over her as she grew. I turned to the sizzling griddle, pulling away from his embrace. "I'll not have you burning the cakes," I pretended to scold.

We sat at the table together, me with less appetite for food as I proudly devoured the vision seated across from me. He held a favored place in the councils of our warrior king, enjoyed great respect from his fellows. Men from all over the kingdom curried his favor and advice. Yet he lavished me and our children with careful attention. Under his hand, our fields and livestock prospered.

I had never so fully appreciated all it meant to be a man or how fully Bedwyr formed the perfect example. I thought I couldn't have loved him more, and yet, in this moment, I did.

With his hair tied back, the strong lines of his jaw and

cheekbones caused me to marvel. How could any man be so well formed? Everything about him pleased me—his big hands, powerful arms, the slope of his neck to the muscled lines of his shoulders. How could I want him so much, mere moments after the rich hours of sex we had enjoyed? After all our years?

But I did. I wanted to fill him with pleasure, feed him my love, until he soared above the battlefield with the powers of the old gods. I wanted his lineage preserved forever. I nestled my belly in my hand, hoping another child would help ensure his essence lived beyond our days.

I refilled his bowl and cooked more bread, lingering at his side so that my palm might trace the curves of his sturdy back. My eyes feasted on the expressions crossing his face, this face I knew so well, that I dreamed of and longed for through long, lonely weeks. His eyes told of heinous scenes, men wounded and dying, gruesome cries of the battlefield, the gore washed off wounds until streams ran red.

A fierce anger seized me at the thought of him being struck down, his lifeblood spilled under the boots of strangers. I would take the sword myself to protect him.

"They may defeat us," he warned, his voice suddenly quiet. The room shivered around us. "They still come," he added tiredly, "a never-ending stream. And our fellow Britons continue to die."

A frightened pulse skidded in my neck. He had never spoken so grimly of our prospects. Always he had been full of hope and challenge.

"We'll fight to the last man, if we must," he continued, "but only if we see some chance of success. We've agreed to pull back and save ourselves if they will overrun us, if they will come west and find our homes." His eyes glimmered at me. "Our women."

"Surely…" I began.

He shook his head. "They're savages. We know what they'll do."

Fear grew at his words. I saw what he faced, what we all faced, and I had nothing to offer, no man's strength for fighting, no magic of the old ways. Much of our ancient power, our religion and priests, had been destroyed by the Romans four hundred years before. But instead of freeing us to rebuild our old ways, the Roman withdrawal had simply opened the door to new invasions. But these coarse pale-haired men offered none of the refinements we had learned from the Romans, only brutality and death.

"I'll make an offering at the spring before I leave," I said, trying to reassure myself as much as him. "They'll not come this far west, Bedwyr, I'm sure of it."

He smiled, leaning back and resting his hands on the table. "Much as I'm strengthened in seeing you again, it eases my mind that you join the others." He raised his hand at my unuttered protest. "If I can't return, if I can't defend you…"

Lines of worry marked his face and his eyes met mine.

"I need to know you're safe," he finished.

He stood up, covering himself in the leather, his cloak, the weapons. I wrapped the last of the flat bread in a cloth, along with a clutch of summer plums and the last of my honey cake. His horse grazed near the creek, and I followed him down the slope, resisting my fear and my own selfish need to keep him by my side.

With the foodstuffs added to his saddle pack, he turned to me. I couldn't bear it, to see him go, to know what he faced. He brushed the tears off my cheeks and held me wrapped close to his chest.

"Don't be afraid," he whispered. "I'll be back."

"I'll be waiting," I mumbled against his scarred battle vest.

He heaved himself onto the tall horse and adjusted his weapons. With a smile that will always stay in my memory, he turned. Water flew up as they crossed the creek, the horse's haunches glistening in the afternoon sun. I watched as they crested the ridge, as he kicked the horse to gallop, until the image of their dark form melted into the line of the land.

THE PROMISE OF MEMORY

Regina Kammer

Imperial Palace, Rome, 100 AD

*A*elia guided the shuttle slowly through the fine linen warp, deftly tamping the threads to form the thin, delicate cloth. The fabric was sheer, Rome's bright sunlight revealing the shadow of the standing loom through the finished work pulled taut by heavy stone weights.

She tensed at the sound of leather soles slapping against the terra-cotta tiles of the breezeway, echoing boldly through the atrium, the familiar foot treads of half a dozen men, one stronger, more self-assured than the others.

Him and his entourage: a knight of the equestrian order with his loyal legionaries.

As she always did, Aelia looked up as he strode by. His tanned, battle-honed arms swung at his sides in cadence to the sway of his short, striped tunic brushing his robust thighs. The leather straps of his sandals strained around the bulk of his calves. Silvered scars from short swords and spearheads marred his limbs, testaments to his prowess in the emperor's provincial campaigns. His light-brown hair was only slightly darker than that of his blond Batavian bodyguards, distant kinsmen to Aelia's own tribe, their coloring matching hers, reminding her with their every visit of her native Germania and of her past.

And, as the knight always did, he looked into her weaving room and nodded slightly, offering a heartfelt smile, while a faraway glint, almost nostalgic, sparkled in his eyes.

But he never came to the palace to see her.

It was no secret the empress had a lover. The emperor himself was busy with the palace *pueri*, boys specially trained in the imperial *paedagogium* to fulfill his every want and need, from curling his hair, to pouring his wine, to decorating his atrium, to satisfying him in bed. Not to be outdone by her husband, the empress had mined the ranks of the *equites* for her perfect lover. These knights of the Roman army strengthened their bodies in the emperor's perpetual wars, their unmarried state ensuring their hunger for female flesh, their unique career *cursus* feeding their material ambitions and solidifying their loyalty to the crown. Subordinate to the senators in the *ordo* of Roman society, the equestrians could never harbor aspirations for the throne, but as guardians of finance and territory, they were able to procure personal wealth rivaling that of the imperial family. They were men of strength, men of ambition, men of valor. Irresistible to a woman of power still in her prime.

The empress's knight came to her apartments in the palace three times a week, two nights and one afternoon, passing along the same passageways, passing before the open doorway of Aelia's weaving room.

The empress's wails of ecstasy had revealed his name. Manius—*morning*—his presence sweeping through the palace corridors like the rising sun, a beckoning brightness to Aelia's otherwise tedious life. A name that evoked memories of her husband, Tagaulf—*daylight*—captured during the Roman onslaught along the Rhine, his final words to her, "I will find you, Austrud. Wait for me. I will find you."

But that had been over ten years ago. She was no longer called by her Chatti name, but had been given a Roman *nomen* when she was bound to the imperial household. And while her heart still waited, her head knew the truth. Tagaulf was surely dead, massacred along with her countrymen in a frenzy of Roman blood thirst.

But the presence of the *eques* confused that certainty. With his smile, she saw Tagaulf's grin. The twinkle in his eye teased her like her husband's had. She reminded herself the two men were so very different. The clean-shaven cheeks and close-cropped hair of the knight, his brawny musculature, his mature confidence, all were in stark contrast to the shaggy hair and wispy beard of the lean, boyish Tagaulf. Yet both roiled her senses, and in the case of the living, breathing Manius, it was to utter distraction.

Only once had she seen the knight face-to-face and touched his masculine warmth. One afternoon, returning from the drying rooms of the dyers, she carried twisted hanks of spun linen in her arms, realizing, by the time she reached the breezeway before her studio, there were too many to hold. The uppermost hanks fell to the tiles, and she tried, vainly, to hold on to the rest as she bent down to pick up the scattered bundles. Suddenly, he appeared, unnoticed as he often was after exiting the empress's bedchamber, his steps more languid, less demanding than when he had arrived earlier that afternoon.

He crouched to her level and reached for the hank of

gray-blue at the same time she did, his strong fingers encircling hers, the heat of his palm spreading through her body like wildfire. Her face flushed, matching, she was sure, the deep crimson stripes of his tunic. She dared to look him in the eyes, the same color as the recalcitrant linen, the blue-gray of the summer sky in Germania. The color of freedom once held in her youth. The same color as her husband's.

Surprise flitted imperceptibly across his face, turning quickly to enchantment. "Let me help you."

His voice was gravelly, deep, conveying the serenity his body felt after having slaked his need between the empress's legs. He reached for the unbalanced load in her arms, shifting his weight, his short tunic riding up his muscular thighs to reveal he did not wear a *subligaculum* wrapped around his loins. His satisfied cock lay slack against his pendulous balls, then twitched and livened under her captivated gaze.

Her breaths came quickly, excitedly at the sight. She had to look away—at his thighs, at his hands, at his scars, at anything else. Her eyes rested on his face now too close to hers, the corners of his lips curled in amusement and expectation.

And then, as he took her burden from her arms, his hands brushed against her breasts, the band of his gold signet ring tweaking a piqued nipple. He stared admiringly at the sight of the tender peaks tightening in wanton desire.

She tried in vain to control her panting breaths.

He lifted an eyebrow and wetted his lips, holding her eyes firmly with his own.

Her pulse beat furiously, pounding in her head, rushing heat to rouse her sex, wetness to pool between her thighs. And then he stood, before she could think to do the same, his erection tenting the fabric of his tunic before her face.

She licked and parted her lips.

His growl of approval returned her to her senses. She bolted upright as swiftly as her trembling legs would allow, then bowed her head. "Many thanks, my lord knight," she mumbled timorously. "The weaving studio is just here." She indicated her small room, the room with the vantage point of his path to the empress's bedchamber. A room, until that moment when she stood flushed and quivering before him, he had apparently not noticed.

Every day since then he had glanced in her studio as he passed, slowing slightly, looking upon her with desirous eyes on his way to the empress; then, upon his return, with his full mouth spread in a satisfied smile. Every day she glanced back at his handsome visage, square jawed and chiseled, heat rising in her face, fantasies exciting her, making her grow wet, hoping he could read her mind.

Afterward, when he had left, she wondered if she were betraying the memory of her husband. The Chatti revered the married state, unlike the Romans who were far too eager to renege on their vows according to whim or ambition. It was unnatural to dream of stroking a stranger's well-muscled arms as his thick fingers gripped her waist, holding her steady while he took his satisfaction from her body and gave her ecstasy in return. Unnatural, yet so deliciously exciting. Surely her husband would not have wanted her desires to languish unfulfilled?

And with his every encouraging glance, the knight emboldened Aelia to consider how she might see more of him. Once or twice too often she worked in her weaving room late at night in dismal lamplight. Still, it was not enough and her thoughts grew more devious.

Slaves and freedwomen moved unseen in the empress's

rooms, each attending to a particular task to preserve the seamless functioning of the household organization. At night, *cubiculariae* waited at the ready for their mistress's every need in the bedroom, taking turns at the watch, sitting silently as she slept, often dozing off in boredom. One evening, after the sunlight had faded and she could weave no longer, Aelia easily insinuated herself amongst the dozens of attendants.

She discharged a sleepy servant ensconced behind the closed curtain of the bedroom's antechamber. The girl scampered off with gratitude, quite possibly for the opportunity to meet her own lover. Aelia positioned herself with a vantage of the impressive four-poster bed upon which the empress lay naked and waiting, the glow of oil lamps burnishing shadows across her skin and sprinkling highlights through her unbound hair.

And then he entered, flanked by his bodyguards.

The Germans held back at the entrance as Manius tossed aside his mantle, dropped his sword belt, and strode purposefully to his queen.

She smiled and spread her legs, then nodded.

He knew his function, his place. He took off his sandals then knelt on the mattress and lowered his head to the thatch of dark hair covering her sex.

Aelia's eyes widened. Her husband had never done such a thing.

From the empress's reaction, it was most enjoyable. She bucked and squirmed, clutched at the knight's hair, beseeched the gods, cried out his name. Manius feasted and licked like a starving man. He slid his hands under her bottom to push her up, angling her to gain better access.

And then the empress screamed to the heavens.

Aelia looked around nervously, wondering if she should

go to the aid of her mistress. But not even the German guards stirred.

Manius slipped off the bed to stand on the mosaic floor, his aroused prick lifting the hem of his tunic before his hands did the same, revealing the rippled muscles of a fierce soldier. Broad shoulders tapered through a solid core to sculpted hips and thick thighs, a body Heracles himself would envy. Light brown hair—the color betraying his provincial heritage—lay in swirls across his chest and trailed to his crotch, growing darker and thicker at the root of his sex. He remained at attention, straining, tautly pulled, only the glorious length of his twitching cock hinting at the lust raging within.

It was the most magnificent sight Aelia had ever seen.

She sucked in air, the sound of which distracted the knight from his duty momentarily. He flicked his eyes toward the curtain behind which she stood, raising a brow, quashing a grin until it simply looked like a lascivious leer for his queen.

Then, in one swift move, he pulled the empress off the mattress and pushed her face-front against a carved wooden post at the foot of the bed. Her body wavered as he murmured into her ear, rocked his hips against her arse, rubbed his excited cock between her fleshy cheeks.

She was small beside his bulk, vulnerable, trapped, nodding in accession to his commands. She reached up to grab hold of the post above her head, then bent over, offering her backside for his taking.

He wrapped his strong hands on either side of her hips and pulled her toward him. He entered her with a sharp thrust.

She groaned in appreciation, then blasphemed the gods when he pulled out slowly and rammed back in.

Aelia's heart pounded, dizzying her into the realm of fantasy where it was her own slick passage the knight conquered.

The empress gripped the bedpost for dear life as Manius slammed against her, holding on to her hips until he found his rhythm. His cadence established, he relinquished her torso and grabbed her unbound hair, a fistful in each hand, as if the tresses were the reins of a horse, and he were leading the charge into battle. The muscles of his buttocks tensed and released to the beat of their slapping bodies, his panting breaths hard and labored, quickening with every exertion, punctuated by clipped grunts...

Rushing to his culmination in the same way Tagaulf had.

One final wicked thrust and the knight released his queen to pull his cock from her satisfied cunt and spew his emission onto the floor between his feet.

And when it was over, Manius quietly slipped his clothes back on as a handful of female servants came to the aid of their mistress. The union had been merely physical, perfunctory. He hadn't even kissed her. He reserved his emotions for someone else.

Before he strode out, he flashed a glance in Aelia's direction, lifting a brow in suggestion and curiosity.

Her dreams that night and every night thereafter were fretful, agitated, filled with memories and possibilities, touching the long blond hair and down-covered skin of her husband, but seeing the chiseled face of Manius, feeling his thick hands grip her forcefully, the weight of him holding her down.

And in the daylight, she feared her dreams betrayed her to the knight. He returned her blushes with knowing smiles.

One night, as was his right, but not necessarily his predilection, the emperor called for the empress to join him in his bed. It was a rare occurrence, simply to keep up appearances, and, on this night, as had happened on all the other occasions, there was no warning.

The empress had muttered an oath to the gods. It was her night with Manius.

It was too late to send word to the *eques*. He would come and find his time wasted.

Unless...

Aelia had access to the empress's bedchamber. She knew all the servants. Half of them would be with their mistress, the other half would relish a respite for one night.

And Manius would need satisfaction.

She had only seen what transpired between them the one time, but she knew what to do. Her heart thumped loudly in her ears as she unbraided her hair. Her hands trembled as she took off her clothes. Still, she had the presence of mind to blow out the lamps. Worries bombarded her as she lay on the bed. Would the empress be relieved early of her wifely duty? Would one of the servants give her away? Would Manius come? What if word had reached him? How long should she wait?

She pulled up a sheet against the chill of the night...

The bang of the door and the thud of footsteps woke her. Manius spoke hushed commands in a guttural tongue to his guards. He strode forward in the dark, knowing how many steps it took to reach the bed, discarding fabric and leather onto the floor. He reached the bed, felt her feet under the sheet, then tore it off, fanning Aelia's fevered skin with a rush of cool air.

His thick hands spanned her calves. He hesitated a moment. Did he sense the woman before him was not who she was supposed to be? A sound—a sigh? a chuckle?—escaped his lips, then he pulled her toward him, spread her legs and bent over her.

The wet heat of his tongue sent shock waves of pleasure to thrill her, tingling all the way to her extremities. She bucked against him, but was held steady by rough hands on each of her ankles. The knight himself dug his fingers and nails into the soft flesh of her bottom to press the depths of her to his mouth to torment her more fully, sucking and licking sensitive parts she never knew she had.

She dared not make a sound, fearing he would stop, fearing his disdain for her betrayal of their mistress. Her breaths puffed rapidly as she struggled to muffle her cries, her strangled gasps seemingly urging him to feast upon her more assiduously. His lavishing tongue roiled the smoldering desire in her core, igniting her lust until it burst forth unexpectedly, a choked cry escaping from her throat, her hips bucking up, demanding more.

And then he stopped. A strike of flint against steel sparked. An oil lamp flared alight.

He stood at the foot of the bed, one brow raised in approbation, his lips curled in delight. Shadows accentuated the deep sculpting of his chest and abdomen, highlights glinted off his expectant cock. On either side of the bed were two German guards awaiting their master's commands. They spread her open and bound her legs to the bedposts with leather straps. The knight reached down and tickled the exposed, wet flesh between her thighs. She flinched, the tug of the bindings and the presence of his bodyguards heightening her vulnerability.

"You are so wet, so wondrously, beautifully wet." He stroked her clitoris slowly, excruciatingly so. "Is all this for me?" he intoned.

Yes, she wanted to say. She opened her mouth but could not answer. He was provoking her to the verge of rapture, to a place where there were no words.

He grinned, reading the acquiescence in her eyes.

Never relinquishing her clit, he climbed over her until he straddled her, his balls rubbing between her breasts, the hair of his thighs chafing her aroused nipples, his knees trapping her arms along her sides. He jutted his cock at her mouth. "Do you want this?"

The gods knew she did, yet would not give her speech. She reached out with her tongue, but he twitched away with a chuckle. She raised her head, straining to lick the musky dew wetting the head of his shaft, succeeding in wrapping her lips around the tip.

He succumbed with an exhale, letting her take him into her mouth, his relentless finger faltering momentarily in his own ecstasy.

She knew what to do. Her husband had relished such attention and had taught her, instruction that Manius seemed to appreciate now. He breathed the same encouragements and satisfactions.

The very same.

She cast him a curious glance.

He pulled away abruptly, returning to stand at the foot of the bed, yet never once breaking his intimate contact. He rubbed her bud with greater alacrity, then inserted two thick fingers inside her.

Aelia clenched around him with a moan.

His eyes widened in victorious delight, then flicked attention to his guards. As he proceeded to penetrate her, his men moved into position. He nodded.

On either side of her a guardsman swooped down to take a nipple in his mouth.

She gasped at the double attack and its unnerving pleasure. They assaulted her with teeth, tongue and hand, sucking, nipping, massaging, thrilling her above as Manius continued to thrill her with his fingers below, his strokes and thrusts more determined.

He held her gaze with his own. "Come." His expression softened, molding his features into a face almost familiar. "Come for me, Austrud."

How could he possibly know that name? How—

Realization jolted her as the crashing waves of culmination drowned her senses. She cried out and thrashed beneath the three men, never taking her eyes off the *eques*.

At the toss of their commander's hand, the Germans stood back and at attention. The knight pulled his fingers away, leaving her bereft but satisfied. He nodded again to his guards, and they began releasing her bindings.

Her breath calmed, clearing her mind, enabling her to compose her thoughts. She dared speak, but what to say? "I am no longer called that," she blurted.

He watched cautiously as the Germans gently placed her unbound feet onto the mattress. "Out," he said when they had finished. "Both of you. Out."

His guards scurried across the mosaic floor to exit the chamber.

And when they were alone, the knight extended himself over her to kiss her mouth with intensity and need.

Aelia's eyes smarted with emotion as she opened for him, wrapping her arms around his shoulders, her legs around his hips. He plumbed her depths, tangled with her tongue, caressed her cheeks.

Just like he used to do.

He broke away and gazed at her from behind dampened

lashes. He entered her yearning passage with a sated groan, relief and contentment coloring his expression. She was tight and unused and he filled her, deliciously so. He moved slowly, instantly aware she had never been with any other man but him.

"Say my name," he murmured, trailing kisses down her neck. "I want to hear you say my name."

She sucked in a strengthening breath. "Tagaulf." Sobs cracked her voice.

He pulled her up and lifted her onto his lap, thrusting into her with a familiar rhythm as his strong arms secured her shaking body.

She cupped his head in her hands looking through tears for traces of the youth she once knew, finding instead scars and creases. "You are so changed."

"I've lived a soldier's life." He rocked his hips, desire straining his expression with every determined stroke. "It broke my body and tried to crush my soul." He weighed a breast in his hand. "You are changed as well." He lowered his head to swirl his tongue around a nipple. "No longer a skinny girl." He bit the peak and growled at her pulsating response. "Instead, a delectable woman."

She rode him, clutching for dear life, trying to savor the shared moment, but desperately needing the shared release.

He gazed at her, his blue-gray eyes red with remembrance. "My wife, my beautiful wife."

His rhythm increased, his thighs and hips lifting and retreating in earnest. He moaned with her body's every response, and she clenched again with his every moan, clutching his well-muscled arms as his thick fingers gripped her waist, holding her steady while he rocked them both toward culmination.

Memories of their days in their native Germania flooded over her...their passionate embraces in the dark forests... frenetic tumbles amidst the valley's spring blossoms. Their days of freedom before the legion under General Trajan's command ravaged their bucolic village, soldiers brutally holding her down as her husband was torn from her side.

She screamed her climax into his chest, shattering the memory of war.

With a clipped cry he plunged himself more deeply inside her, filling her with his seed, with the promise of a new life. For several minutes they held each other tightly, their hearts beating in unison, their breaths still quivering with the recapturing of their blissful past.

With the realization that the man who had destroyed their lives was now emperor, and his wife unwittingly providing a fleeting refuge.

"I feared you dead." Her head nestled in the crook of his neck, her tears streaming down his scarred back.

"I knew they had taken you here." He kissed her hair, inhaling her essence. "I flattered the empress to find you. And then the gods revealed you to me." His voice trembled with restrained emotions. "I broke our vows, and for that I repent every hour of every day of my life." His tears surged forth. "Forgive me, Austrud, forgive my transgression. It was the only way to find you."

He did not love his queen. He did not kiss her, did not take her to the point where two people united as one, their souls entwining and surging to the heavens. "I forgive you, Tagaulf," she said earnestly. "But how did you survive?" She wiped a droplet of sweat from his brow. "I saw our men killed."

He smiled and kissed her lips. "After I was captured, I

made myself indispensable to a tribune." His fingers traveled up her spine, marking every vertebra, remembering her flesh. "He forged my background. Gave me rank beyond my expectations, beyond what our Roman masters would ever allow for us." He threaded his fingers through her hair, smoothing the strands from her glowing face. "I'm respected now. I've money now. I've connections now. In the highest echelons of Rome."

Indeed. The very empress herself.

"I've made an offer for your freedom. I came here tonight expecting the answer."

She saw her own joy reflected in his eyes.

"Austrud, I am forbidden to take you as my wife under their laws." He enveloped her in his arms. "But we know the truth of our past." He inhaled deeply, his chest pressing against hers, the hair tickling her still-sensitive breasts.

"A life with you in any manner is better than a life alone." She slumped against him, her body shaking in sobs of relief and disbelief.

"It will be very soon, my love," he murmured, kissing her forehead. "Be ready at a moment's notice. I will come for you. I promise."

Until that time, knowing her husband was still alive, that he loved her, would be enough to sustain her.

His cock livened inside her, his hips rolled instinctually.

"It's been so long," she breathed. "The gods know I've missed this."

"We've not much time before the household guards grows suspicious."

She smiled and raised a brow in challenge. "Then be Manius for me."

He laughed. "I see. You thought me a cunt-starved *eques* wanting to brutishly ravish the household slaves?"

"Thought, my lord? Rather, I prayed to the gods that you were so."

He grinned. "Inconstant wench, let me show you how a soldier fucks after battle."

With strong arms he flipped her effortlessly onto her stomach, then dug his nails into her hips to spread her wide, opening her for his invasion, crowing at her traitorous wetness. He impaled her with his iron-hard cock, ramming in to the hilt, driving in even more deeply to subdue her squirming form. Satisfied with her subjugation, he plowed into her, concerned only for his release, pressing her face into the mattress to muffle her screams, his own syncopated grunts measuring the march of his inexorable victory. She roared her orgasm, capturing his cock, unwilling to capitulate.

But she was no match for him. He jerked against her, growling, jetting his hot come to sear her inside, branding her as his conquest.

She breathed a sigh of surrender, content in the knowledge that she would share her future with both her loving husband and her virile knight.

On My Honor

Beatrix Ellroy

The Parish of Norwich, England, 1452 AD

Hedda heard a noise. She halted her work, the rich scent of the rosemary rising up, and held her breath, listening carefully. She could hear the distinct metal grind and clank of an armored man walking nearby. She wiped her hands on her apron and peered through the door—a lone knight was stumbling along the lane.

"Good day, Sir Knight. Are you wounded?" she called from the doorway.

"I am lass, I am. But I'm on my way to my Lord Elis and I must get there." He looked over his shoulder. "Is there a church close by to claim sanctuary?"

Hedda shook her head. "The closest church is a quarter-day's walk over the hills." By his labored gait, she guessed the journey would take him closer to half a day and Lord Elis's hold a week or more.

He looked disappointed, and closed his eyes briefly before

visibly straightening and continuing to walk.

"Sir Knight, wait!" Hedda called. She picked up her skirts and ran after him. "Sir Knight, may I offer you succor? The church is far, that is true, but let me ease your wounds." She was bound to offer that much.

As she came closer, she could see a hint of red in his short beard, dark circles beneath his eyes and a rising sun stamped into his breastplate.

There was darkness in his eyes as he looked her over. "I would be humbled lass. I am Sir Cephas, sworn to the service of Lord Elis."

Hedda sketched a curtsey. "I am Hedda. Come inside, Sir Cephas, and tell me of your wounds."

He limped with her to the hut, ducking his head to move inside and lean against the lintel. "Well lass, I was traveling to Lord Elis with news of the battle across the sea when we were set upon. They crippled my horse, and my squire ran, but I managed to defeat the miscreants." His glower made his features fierce. "I have been walking for days and have not removed my plate, so I cannot tell you more than the ache that fires my shoulder and the pain in my knee are the worst."

"I will need you to take off your armor, good Sir, so that I could see your wounds myself."

The knight shook his head. "I would not disrobe so in front of you."

She shook her head at his stubbornness. "I cannot see your wounds through steel."

He pushed himself away from the door. "I will walk to this church you spoke of."

Hedda moved to block the door. "No, Sir Cephas. I am

charged by God to assist those in need. It is no dishonor, to you or me."

"My vows say otherwise."

Hedda narrowed her eyes and stood close to the knight as he looked down and met her gaze. She reached up and pushed him in the chest, and he stumbled backward. "Sit!"

"No."

Her lips narrowed and she pushed again, harder, and leaned into the tall man.

He stumbled and fell back to lean on the table.

Before she could move he caught her hand, the metal of his gauntlet carving into her skin, cold and hard. "Do not do that again, Hedda." His voice held no warmth now.

"Then do as you are told and be still. I'll look at your shoulder first." Her own tone was as cold as his. *Stubborn man.* She began to peel back the straps and buckles of the gauntlet.

The knight moved as if to stand again.

Hedda sighed and leaned into his shoulder, pressing her own leg outward to shift his knee. She felt his sudden intake of breath and smiled tightly. "Be still, Sir Cephas, and this will go much easier."

She peeled off his plate: gauntlets and bracers, pauldrons and breastplate. Her hair fell forward brushing against him as she placed each piece gently on the table. He wore chain and a padded tunic beneath the beaten steel. With a muted grunt of pain, he brought up his arms, and she pulled the chain over his head and let it drop heavily on the floor.

He kept his head down for a moment, breathing hard, and Hedda reached out to touch the purpling bruise rising up from the neck of his padded tunic. She could feel him shiver beneath her fingers as she undid the fastenings and drew the garment over his head, along with the simple undertunic he wore beneath.

She swallowed, suddenly and awfully aware of the knight's body. Usually she healed men with nothing more than an eye for their wounds. Today, her gaze was drawn to Sir Cephas's skin, mottled with bruises; the hair of his chest was matted with sweat and the musky smell of him rose heavy in the room.

"Sometimes, shoulders go the wrong way." She curved her hand around the joint, probing it, waiting to hear the hiss of pain. "This will hurt, but it should also help."

She sent a brief prayer upward, begging forgiveness for the traitorousness of her body and for God's grace in her next act. Swiftly, she brought her hands around his arm, pulling it up and out, feeling the unsettling crack of the joint and hearing Cephas's sharp breath. She stroked over the skin gently, making sure it felt as it should. She breathed deep and cursed inside as the musk of him rose again.

"Many thanks lass. Now, if you could help me don my armor again...?"

She shook her head. "Nay, Sir Knight, I would see this knee wound first."

"You would see me naked?"

"You can keep your breechcloth on."

Their eyes met for a tense moment. When he offered no more complaints, Hedda sighed, then knelt at his feet and began to undo his greaves.

He echoed her sigh and laid his sword on the table. "It should be I who kneels at a maiden's feet, not the other way around."

"Maiden?" Hedda snorted. "I'm no maiden, Sir Cephas. An honest widow, aye, so your form is no surprise to me." She pulled the armor off and laid it to the side, then began to unlace the breeches. "Just keep your breechcloth on and all will be well."

She hoped that the knight could not see the blush beginning to rise on her cheeks as she pulled the cloth and padding from his legs, her gaze lingering on the lengths of hard muscle, marked here and there by scars. His knee was swollen and red, but nothing like the empurpled rage of his shoulder. She rose and went to the shelf beside the door and selected a pot. "I'll apply this salve to your shoulder and your knee, once you've bathed." She eyed the small cuts where his chain had broken the skin. "I want no dirty wound to take you." She stoked the fire and dragged a tub from outside the door and began to haul in water from the well.

The knight rose, still in his breeches that were unlaced to above the knee. "I will help, lass."

Once the buckets were heating over the fire, Hedda donned her cloak and walked into the forest with a promise to be back by sunset. Out in the woods, she prayed over and over for God to take the sinful visions from her mind, but still they lurked. Sir Cephas's broad shoulders, the dark of his beard against his skin. The vise of his fingers around her wrist, daring her to challenge him.

She took a deep breath, tasting the leaves and the air and the coming balance of the equinox marking a descent into the long winter, and turned back for home as the rays of light thinned and faded.

When she ducked through the door, calling the knight's name, she stopped still at the tableau; Sir Cephas was still in the bath, curled up beneath the water, his head resting awkwardly on the edge of the tub. The water turned his hair black, and sleep smoothed the pain lines and the fierceness of his brow. She put the basket on the ground then stood an arm's length from the tub, looking down at him, down at his water-distorted body.

"Sir Cephas," she called softly.

He murmured something, and she leaned closer, willing herself not to look at his body and failing, her eyes drinking in the long lines, the muscles.

She touched him gently on his uninjured shoulder, and in a louder voice said "Wake, Sir Knight."

He burst into movement with a suddenness that made her jump back. He rose and vaulted from the tub, smoothly in spite of the wounds to his knee and shoulder, and the water sheeted from him to fall to the rushes lining the floor.

Hedda covered her eyes and spun to face away from the warrior, but not before noticing the dark hair that furred from his chest to his groin, his manhood hanging heavy and limp between his legs. She felt her blood rise to her skin, her entire body aflame.

"Hedda!" His voice thundered and he rummaged around, grabbing a blanket from her bed and presumably wrapping it around himself. "The dishonor."

Hedda kept her eyes on the wall in front of her with her hands on her hips. "Sir Knight, you were asleep and I woke you. I meant no dishonor, no sin." She offered a dual prayer for forgiveness—for the sin and the lie.

"What you meant has no bearing on what you have done. You shame yourself, woman."

"Shame myself?" Hedda's voice rose in pitch. "I do no such thing, Sir Cephas. I am assisting to heal you, as I vowed to Our Lord. Any shame here is your own, good Sir."

"You come in here while I am unclothed, yet the shame is mine?"

"I did not know you were unclothed until I came in. And any shame is outweighed by my concern that, should you sleep longer in the cold, it will unbalance your humors." She turned then, keeping her eyes on his. "I am no stranger to a man's form, Sir Knight, that is true, but your wounds are what I am more concerned with."

The knight's dark eyes blazed as he stared at her, the softness on his face gone. "Very well." He growled, shifting the blanket around his hips.

With effort Hedda kept her glance on his until a shiver wracked his form. She turned away again and rummaged through a chest before pushing a set of clothes at him and turning back to lock her gaze on the wall where herbs were drying in bunches.

"I doubt they will fit you well but it is enough until your other things dry."

"I cannot spare more time; I must get to Lord Elis."

"It is a week, probably more, to Lord Elis's hold. Longer in your current state. Rest here, bide the night, and leave in the morn. I can help you somewhat with provisions and salves for your wounds. You will make better time after resting than you would walking until you collapse."

He sighed but seemed to acknowledge her point. When he began to drag the tub to the door, she turned. She had been correct; the clothing did not fit well, straining across the knight's shoulders, breeches tight over his thighs. Working in silence they hung the clothes and began the evening meal. As the sun set, Sir Cephas sat again and Hedda picked up the pot of salve.

"I need to rub this into your wounds."

The knight's eyes met hers for a moment, and she cursed

the sudden flash of heat that ran through her, certain it showed in her eyes. He paused then nodded and she knelt before him, undoing the laces of his breeches and baring his thighs.

As she rubbed the scented salve over his flesh he spoke again. "So, Widow Hedda, why do you live so far from the village?"

The knight's voice was softer than before, and he looked genuinely curious.

"Three years past I decided to enter the woods in contemplation, and practice healing where I could."

"Were you not a healer before?"

"Not really. I helped the midwife sometimes, but mostly my late husband and I kept the farm."

"Does it not worry you, being so far from the village?"

"Only that should something happen, I will have no help. I get visitors when someone needs my help, and sometimes the priest will send a parishioner to me for a month."

"Is it not lonely?"

"Oh, yes." Hedda breathed the words then regretted the naked longing and cleared her throat. "Yes, it can be lonely, but 'tis no real hardship." She continued rubbing her hands over his knee.

"It is no place for a woman, not even with the grace of God." He sounded disapproving.

Hedda stood, hands on her hips, and looked down at the knight. "I need no keeper. You're the most dangerous visitor I've had, Sir Knight." Her voice was harsher than she meant it to be.

Cephas's dark eyes met hers, pools of black in the firelight. "I'm no knave, I do not mean to treat you poorly, be you maiden or widow."

Hedda looked away then silently drew his tunic down to

bare his shoulder and began to smooth the salve into his skin. She remained silent for several long moments with only the crack and snap of the fire.

Finally she spoke, her hands still gently stroking over his skin. "I do not doubt your honor, Sir Knight, or your intent. And if I did, I could run faster than you."

"I would catch you, eventually." He stood and loomed over her.

"You're certain of that?" Hedda met his gaze and pushed her palm into his shoulder again. "It would only be if I let you."

He grunted slightly and caught her wrist firmly again. "I told you not to do that." He growled, tightening his grip enough to make her wince.

She jutted her chin. "Or what Sir Knight?"

He pushed her backward into the wall, the drying herbs crushed behind her shoulders, releasing a sudden scent of rosemary and thyme into the air. He towered over her, and she caught her breath, balanced between fear and desire, chest heaving, and she could feel her dress tighten across her breasts. She opened her mouth to speak but could form no words. He pushed her harder into the wall, his hand clamped across her wrist, and she arched toward him.

"What do you mean to do with me now that you've caught me?" She licked her lips, breathless.

His eyes followed her tongue, glancing at her breasts, and then he bared his teeth and moved away, dropping her hand. "Nothing. I will do *nothing*. You tempt me beyond reason."

She flushed red then, unable to speak.

"Why entice me so?" His voice was anguished. "The Lord calls us to fidelity, to honor."

Hedda found her voice, creaky with tears as it was. "I do

not do this to seduce you. I did not mean to upset you."

"Then why? Why provoke me like this?" He touched his shoulder.

"I do not know," she said, bowing her head. "I have been a long time alone."

"You've had visitors; you've healed others."

"None like you, Sir Cephas." She shrugged. "Oh, some are as well made, as honorable, as stoic. But none are like you."

Her shame rose and broke, like a wave, unable to rise higher. Instead, she took two steps to stand close to him, close enough to smell the sharpness of the rosemary and arnica in the balm on his shoulder and knee.

He did not move but watched her, carefully. She thought of the winter coming upon her, on that last careful celebration before the long nights descended.

"You strain my honor, woman, my temper," he said hoarsely.

"On this night, Sir Cephas, this night between the autumn and the winter, think of a different honor. Think of the long winter and the last harvest and taking what pleasure we can." She spoke in low tones and took the last step to stand brushing against him. "Would you give me this, a memory to warm me come winter?" She watched his throat work, patterns of light and dark in the firelight, the smell of rosemary rising up all around them.

"You wish to shatter my honor?" he said, voice raw. "To break me of my word?"

His arms moved around her, and she breathed out in a sigh. He swallowed it down, his mouth on hers like a brand, the heat making her skin prickle. His beard rubbed against the softness of her skin as his lips, his tongue moved on hers, and she rose to her toes, her own hands circling around him, beneath the rough cloth of his tunic to press against the skin beneath.

He moaned into her mouth. "Hedda, I…"

"Shhh." She drew him back down for a kiss, walking backward with him to bump against her bed. "Lay, Sir Cephas, let me…" She stumbled over the words. For all her longing and desires, this was almost entirely new; she had rutted before, but not like this.

She acted instead, pushing him down and kneeling over him, her inner thighs pressing against the hard lines of his hips, her hair hanging around them like a curtain. His hands clutched her flesh, and she lowered herself to press against him.

His manhood was fiercely hard, even through his breeches and her skirts. His moan was muffled, and she closed her eyes for a moment.

"Hedda." His voice was broken, and raw. "I cannot lie with you; I will not." His hips thrust against her in spite of his words. "I would leave no bastards behind; I would not shame you so."

She rested her hands together on his belly, feeling the muscles move and bunch beneath his tunic before pushing it up to touch flesh against flesh, skin against skin, drinking in the sensation, her hands still soft with salve. She opened her eyes to see Cephas's face, the shadow and light obscuring all but the anguish there. She whimpered as the firmness of his member pushed between her thighs and her own body slicked in response.

"We, ah, we do not have to…" She paused and took a breath. "We do not have to lie together in that manner."

With enormous effort she let her hips roll only once before moving to stand again. "We can be together, but not lay together. I desire you, Sir Knight, but I would not harm you or your honor."

He rolled to sit on the bed facing her. "What do you mean, Hedda?"

She looked him in the eye and stepped between his knees, drawing his face to hers. "Spend your seed upon my belly, my breasts, my mouth. Touch me, within and out." She closed the gap and pressed her mouth to his, their lips soft and pliant, breath fast and unsteady. "Kiss me where you wish. Just do not ride me."

His hands rose to sit gentle upon her waist, his thumbs resting against the laces of her dress. "I would see you, Hedda, bare in this light." The knight's voice was husky. "I wish to draw these clothes from you, and see you laid naked before me."

His touches set her skin aflame. The barest of whispers as he undid laces, drew fabric down and away, fingertips barely brushing her until she stood completely naked in the firelight. His hands clenched hard on her shoulders as he said her name, a plea and a prayer: "Hedda."

Then his mouth descended upon hers, swallowing her moans as his hands roamed. Her own fingers, clever and quick, unlaced tunic and breeches, let them drop and drew them over, until he was as bare as her. The firelight danced over them, the crackle and spit of the fire a counterpoint to their breaths and moans.

"Lie down again, Sir Cephas." Hedda looked at him, eyes vivid behind the curtain of her hair. "Let me do this for you."

The knight shuddered against her as she spoke, and he lay back down, his manhood spearing out hard from the hair between his thighs. She drew her hands over him, through the hair, over his skin, from the still-swollen knee to the violent purple of his shoulder, to his beard and his hair in disarray. She danced her hand along his cock, stroking lightly, until his own hand rose to join hers, firmly. She twisted her wrist to grasp his hand, and climbed to kneel over his prone form.

"Not yet, Sir, I beg of you."

She dipped down to let her body brush against the flesh of his manhood, the skin and hair. Her own body flexed and tingled at the sensations driven by her movement down, her face close to the juncture of his thighs. Her tongue, sly and pink, flicked out to taste along his length.

"Oh God in Heaven," the knight swore. "Hedda."

"Shhhhh," she murmured against his skin, and he moaned, close to a sob. She gripped him with both hands, her mouth closing around the very tip of him, and his body went stiff, hips flexing upward. Before she could do much more than suckle at him, his hands gripped her shoulders and pulled her, pushed her, to lie beside him on the bed, where he kissed her again, using his teeth and his tongue.

"I fear I cannot kneel over you as you knelt over me," he said, mouth against her neck.

She shivered as his teeth pressed against her skin.

"But you could kneel over me in a different manner."

Even though his shoulder afforded him little movement, he still managed to pull her upward again, her knees spread wide and awkward until his tongue touched against her and she choked out a sob.

"Cephas!"

His tongue touched again and she keened, low beneath her breath, and her hips shifted. His good arm moved and his fingers probed her entrance; one slipped into her.

She moaned. "Jesus help me."

The knight's finger moved, entering her over and over until, the slickness wetting her thighs, he pushed a second into her. She moaned and swore and she could feel his mouth curve into a smile against her center, making her slicken and flex all the more. She felt joy rising, pushing at her, drawing everything to her, until his teeth closed upon the soft flesh of her thigh.

She sobbed in frustration. "Sir, Cephas, please," she begged. "Do not stop."

"I wish to try something else, lass."

He pulled at her again, pushing her, positioning her limbs, until she lay atop him, facing up to the ceiling, his member hard beneath her bottom. His legs rose between hers, pulling her knees apart and she blushed at the wanton display, then his fingers moved against her again, and she squirmed.

"That's it, lass." His voice was low, breath moving against her ear. "Writhe against me."

Hedda whimpered, her skin aflame, a shocked moan escaping as he pulled at one nipple then the other. His palm flattened over her mound, and she thrust up against it. The knight pulled it away, reaching between her spread thighs to move his cock to thrust up against her wetness, lying against her but not inside her. It jutted up from her own body, obscene and huge. Sir Cephas's legs moved again, trapping hers between them and pressing her thighs closed, tightly.

When he began to thrust up between her thighs and her wetness, they both moaned out loud. She moved her hand down to feel his cock pushing out from her own mound, pressing her fingers into the wetness to caress the bud hidden there. A few strokes, and she felt the wave rise once more, the joy swallowing her as she came, legs quivering around the knight's hard shaft and her body flexing against his.

Cephas moaned and thrust harder and faster, until he began to spend between her thighs, his seed thick and white against the darkness of her hair. His hand spread the seed upward, over the soft flesh of her belly.

"Hedda," he murmured, rolling over to nestle her into his side. "I do not think that was precisely what my Order allows, but..." He laid a line of sweet kisses upon her neck. "I honor you nonetheless."

For the rest of the evening they moved around each other with exaggerated care, eating quietly and retiring to the small, narrow bed together. He was hard again, pressing against her belly as they kissed until she felt drunk on it, until she keened as she ground herself against his thigh.

His enormous hand curved around her hip, pulling her leg up until he could reach between her thighs and push two fingers into the slickness. As she moaned, he took his hand away and pushed her onto her back and rose over her on his good shoulder to part her thighs and push his fingers back into her again, his thumb on her pearl, until she came again weeping his name. He used her wetness to jack himself until he spent between her breasts, pushing one slick finger between her lips and crying out as she suckled at it.

Afterward, Hedda watched the fire settle and die into coals, Cephas's arm encircling her and an ache growing in her chest.

In the morning, she packed a small pouch of cheese and bread, with herbs to sweeten the smell, and then helped him to don his armor, her fingers quick and certain. As she knelt before him, tightening the straps of his greaves, she felt his gauntleted hand rest gently on her head.

"Fare thee well, Sir Knight." She smiled up into his face,

which appeared younger and less pained than it had the day before.

"And thee, milady." The knight leaned down and kissed her fiercely, his armor hard against her soft flesh. "May my travels bring me to your door again," he said gruffly, his gaze locking with hers for a long moment. And then he turned and walked, limping only slightly, back up the lane.

Hedda watched until he was out of sight. Then, straightening her shoulders, she turned back to the cottage. She had much to do and could spare no time mooning over a handsome knight. But as her gaze went to her door, her breath caught and hope bloomed within her chest. For carved hastily into the wood above her door was the crude picture of a sun rising.

A Falcon in Flight

Connie Wilkins

Armenia, during the Mongol Invasion, 1236 AD

Georgia will fall within the year." Father Kristopor drew a careful line across the map before him. "The Mongol hordes spread like a rising sea, though they throw up clouds of dust instead of salt spray."

"They will come here, as well." Ardzvik paced the length of the hall and back. "We will be destroyed in days, however well our few men fight."

"We must pray for another way."

His pious words did not deceive her. The priest's devious turn of mind was legend. She would gladly lead her people in battle, or barricade as many as would fit inside the ancient fortress of Anberd at risk of being starved out, but too many would be lost. If there was a better choice, she must take it.

When word of defeat came from Georgia's capital, Father Kristopor searched out Ardzvik on the mountainside where she hunted with her falcon, Zepyur. She knew, seeing him from far above, what his mission must be, and cursed fate for robbing her of the longed-for solace she reserved for such fine, cloudless days when the blue sky went on above her forever and her falcon soared high and free with no likely prey in sight. At least the priest had not discovered her in the midst of what he would surely consider sin.

"Now is the time," he called, and then, when he was closer, "Send at once to the Mongol general. Say that the Province of Aragatsotn in Armenia has long been a vassal of Georgia, so it is only right that its people offer fealty to the new rulers. I will bear the document myself. The Mongols are quick enough to sack churches, but I have heard that they retain some degree of respect for holy men of any faith."

"Surrender without a battle." The words, bitter on Ardzvik's tongue, burned even more in her heart.

"Without blood. Surely they would rather have the wine of our vineyards and grain of our fields than the lifeblood of those who tend them. Dead men cannot be taxed."

So it was done. Ardzvik Zakaria, Lady of Aragatsotn, signed above the seal presented to her father's father in Tbilisi by the legendary Queen Tamar of Georgia.

As soon as the priest rode his mule northward, Ardzvik retrieved her falcon from the mews and rode again high onto the mountain. Zepyur was still as swift and graceful, the sky as blue, but now the Lady of Aragatsotn could not shed her duty, her constraints, and be pure flesh and spirit.

Lying back on tufted mountain grass, she envisioned, as she had so often, the airborne mating dance of the wild falcon pair that had produced her own sleek hunter, but she could not rid her mind of earthbound turmoil.

Her hands knew all the ways to pleasure herself, the places

to twist or stroke or beat with rough force while a part of her soared aloft with the falcons, the earth dropping away, away, until they plummeted together as one through space. Falling, falling, diving faster than anything could fall, cold air ripping past, battering, the ecstasy forced deeper and deeper, keener, unbearable...and her own ecstasy bursting forth at last like the cataclysm that had torn open the mountain's peak.

But this time, no matter how hard she rubbed or how deeply she probed, she achieved only a sharp burst of sensation, as much pain as pleasure. The scream forced from her throat was of rage, not triumph, and tears flowed hotter on her cheeks than the rivulets of sweet release between her thighs. Surrender without battle. Dishonor. But duty nonetheless.

The Mongol general returned a provisional acceptance and sent men to assess an initial amount of tribute. Within months he was appointed governor, or *darugha* in the Mongol tongue, of southern Georgia and northern Armenia.

Now, weeks later, the mighty Yul Darugha had come to view the corner of his territory dominated by Mount Aragats, the highest point in Armenia.

It was rumored that he toured the land to view more than mountains and plains and vineyards. From priest to priest, monastery to monastery, landholder to landholder, the rumor spread that Batu Khan, grandson of the great Ghengis, had withdrawn to his new city of Sarai on the lower Volga, and encouraged his troops and officials in conquered territory to ensure the Mongol heritage by mingling their blood with that of the local population.

It was rumored as well that the Khan appointed only governors with no family ties of importance in their homeland, the better to ensure their loyalty to him and no other and keep them in their posts. The old nobility, what was left of them, hid their daughters or put them on display, according to their level of ambition. The young Lady of Aragatsotn would neither hide nor put herself forward, whatever her half-sister Leyli might do.

This Mongol's looks intrigued Ardzvik. Perhaps he could even be called handsome if one became accustomed to his shaven head, bold, high cheekbones, and tilted eyes beneath eyebrows with the graceful swoop of a falcon's wing. Muscular, as well, which would please Leyli, and a fine rider, though Leyli's interest in riding did not always involve horses.

Ardzvik sensed the shift in Leyli's mood. One form of tension had yielded to quite another. "So, sweet sister," she murmured, "are you still of a mind to slay this governor should you get the chance?" She would not permit Leyli to do any such thing, of course, bringing the fury of Batu Khan's forces down upon them, as Leyli knew quite well.

"Yes, I will kill him if I can. For the sake of poor Mihran. But...not, I think, right away." Leyli allowed her milk-white mare to fidget under her, enough to draw the Mongol's attention away from Father Kristopor's diplomatic speech of welcome. The man had already surveyed the mare with all the admiration due her, and Leyli too, though less overtly. Now, as the girl peered flirtatiously through lowered eyelashes and fiddled in feigned nervousness with her long golden hair, it seemed that he could scarcely wrench his gaze away.

Ardzvik's own high-bred bay mount had been assessed favorably as well, though she herself elicited a puzzled frown. Just as she had intended. Despite Father Kristopor's disapproval, she was dressed soberly in garb so simple that she might have been mistaken for someone of much lower rank in contrast to Leyli's azure robes gleaming with gold brocade. All the easier to assess his reaction to her half-sister's charms before Ardzvik had cause to care. Not that such a thing was remotely possible.

She had not much cared that "poor Mihran," a minor prince of Georgia sent officially to court her, had lost his heart and whatever virginity he might have had to Leyli instead. Ardzvik was sorry for his death during the fall of Georgia, but not on a personal level. Better she should never care overmuch for any man.

Father Kristopor closed his speech with an offer of the hospitality of the castle as lodging for the Darugha and his men. The interpreter did his part, and the Mongol said a few words in response. The priest signaled for Ardzvik and Leyli and their retinue to advance. They rode forward out of the shadow of the ancient stone church at a stately pace.

This encounter had been staged in the town's center as a diplomatic compromise. The ruling family need not go as supplicants to the Darugha's great golden tent, nor he with his men as conquerors to the gates of their castle. The Lady of Aragatsotn was a vassal, not a slave.

The interpreter, a handsome young man with Persian features, spoke toward the space between Ardzvik's dark head and Leyli's fair one. Good. Father Kristopor had obeyed her order to be deliberately vague as to which was the ruler and which was not. "His Eminence Yul Darugha thanks the Lady of Aragatsotn for her offer of the hospitality of her castle. However, it is his custom to sleep only within his personal tent."

Ardzvik felt the gaze of Yul Darugha sweep over her, linger on her horse, then return to her face. She met his keen eyes, saw that he had not been deceived after all, lifted her chin proudly and spoke not in Armenian but in the basic Turkic tongue most often used between tradesmen in the various countries of the lower Caucasus. "If Yul Darugha pleases, we would offer a feast in his honor tonight, to be held in the gardens of the castle." It was well known by now that the nomadic Mongols were ill at ease confined within rigid walls.

With no pause for instructions, the interpreter began to decline this invitation, too, as expected—the governor had not been known to dine with any of such noble families as remained—but a rich, deep voice startled them all.

"Yul Darugha will be pleased to accept."

That voice penetrated all the way into Ardzvik's bones. For a moment she did not comprehend the words, though they were spoken in the same tongue she had used. So the interpreter had been merely a formality. With an effort, she inclined her head briefly. "We shall be honored by his presence, and that of his men." She looked up to see a hint of amusement on the governor's sun-browned face. Without another word, to her disappointment—why did she wish so to hear that voice again? To feel it?—he turned his dun horse and moved away toward the camp outside the town with his two dozen soldiers following.

"Father Kristopor said the man would never accept the invitation!" Leyli trotted at her side as they turned toward the road to Aragatsotn Castle.

"Yes, he did." The priest had looked more pleased than surprised. Ardzvik would have words with him later. "So now there is much to be done."

"And outdoors—well, it is very warm today, and the sun sets late. But what shall I wear? Did you see how he looked at me? And that voice!"

Ardzvik urged her high-strung horse forward to let him

stretch his legs after standing so long in the town and to leave Leyli's prattle behind.

The castle was built into a rocky outcropping on the lower slopes of Mount Aragats. From its gardens, enclosed by low walls, the wide view swept from rolling fields and wooded valleys in the southeast to the Caucasus mountain range in the northeast, still snowcapped in midsummer. The steward set up trestle tables while Ardzvik worked with the kitchen staff to prepare a creditable meal, not elaborate but representing the best the province offered: lamb rubbed with herbs and grilled on skewers, chicken in walnut sauce, bulgur-stuffed grape leaves and eggplant, and sweet pastries topped with honeyed apricots and cherries.

The Mongol rank-and-file soldiers, when they came, kept largely to themselves at one side, not quite at ease but taking good advantage of the repast, especially the wine from local vineyards. Yul Darugha ate and drank sparingly, needing only occasional recourse to his interpreter to converse with Father Kristopor. A Mongol priest, or shaman in their tongue, sat with them but ate little and rarely spoke. Leyli, though she understood only a few of their words, listened with rapt attention and leaned forward the better to display her bountiful charms.

Ardzvik listened as well when she was not directing the servants, who were flustered by the exotic strangers in their midst. The rise and fall of the governor's deep voice had a hypnotic affect on her, so that only the occasional phrase registered. Father Kristopor, who had traveled extensively in his youth, led the conversation into talk of distant lands, never alluding to the fact that their guests had been in those places for the purpose of pillage and conquest.

"Truly? A real Sultan's palace!" Leyli's high voice jolted

Ardzvik into attention. "Did he have a harem? What did the ladies wear? They would have finer silks than we can purchase here." She took the occasion to stroke the bodice of her own silk gown languidly while the interpreter, stammering a bit, relayed her words.

Ardzvik was not close enough to kick her sister under the table.

Leyli ignored the priest's frown. "The Sultan's ladies must have been much more beautiful than we here to the north," she went on, then stopped abruptly at Yul Darugha's fierce scowl.

"Can you know so little of war?" The deep voice that had flowed so smoothly took on the edge of a scimitar. "The women of the seraglio, taken by surprise, fled in fear for their lives, some wearing little or nothing at all. As to beauty, many had been sold into slavery for the sake of that beauty, especially those few with golden hair such as yours."

Leyli shrank back at the demonic cast to his face.

Ardzvik saw something deeper in his eyes, like the fury of a stallion who has come through great violence and bears invisible scars. She rose and went to stand beside him, wishing she had not thought of stallions.

"Come, Governor," she said, "while there is still light enough, let me point out the villages and places of interest to be seen from here. You must wish to be familiar with the territory under your rule."

"Yes," he said, his face relaxing a degree. "Thank you, Lady Ardzvik."

And she knew his gratitude was as much for the interruption as for her suggestion.

After she had shown him the major towns, they stood together in silence where the low wall curved to the brink of an outcropping and the mountainside dropped steeply away. The sun had edged behind a shoulder of Aragats, but shone still on the distant mountains and gilded their snow-capped peaks.

"Always before," he said at last, "I judged land as to how a battle should be fought, or how many horses could be sustained. Often both. But a governor must learn to look with different eyes." He glanced down at her, then said, as though reading her mind, "No, not merely to plan how much tax can be raised from the flocks and crops and craftsmen before they are bled dry. Your people are well fed and housed, and productive. You understand the long-term value of their well-being."

She forbore to mention that thus far she herself had borne as much of the cost of tribute as possible so that her people would not suffer more than could be helped. Better to lighten his mood further and her own as well. This close to him, the reverberations of his voice and his aura of power affected her so strongly she could barely keep from quivering like a mare in heat when the stallion comes near. How could she be so foolish? "My father and his father before him were good stewards of the land. My family's only taste for extravagance has been in our horses, though I do not keep so many in these times." No need to say how many had been sold to pay the tribute he had levied.

"Take me to see your horses," he said abruptly.

Ardzvik heard movement at the table they had left, along with Leyli's ever-resilient voice raised in laughter, and understood his request. She led him quickly to a gate that gave onto a path leading downhill to a cluster of stables and a fenced field. A dozen horses grazed there, while others, including those of the visiting Mongols, could be seen on a plateau slightly lower on the mountainside.

Leyli's white mare came up to the gate at once, snuffling hopefully for treats. Yul Darugha ran a hand along her neck until she moved petulantly away since nothing edible was forthcoming. "A pretty creature," he said, "like her mistress." He looked to where Ardzvik's blood bay advanced and retreated, wishing to come to his mistress, displeased by the stranger's presence. "But yours, Lady Ardzvik, is the nobler beast by far. A touch of the Arab for grace and beauty." She nodded assent. "I knew at once," he went on, "that the rider of such a mount must be the true ruler here."

Ardzvik felt her face redden at the reminder of her earlier attempt to confuse him. It seemed a good time to redirect the conversation. "Please forgive my half-sister for her foolishness tonight. She is not always so lacking in sense." Defending Leyli to this man was like probing a self-inflicted wound, but it needed to be done.

Some trick of the fading light made Yul Darugha's eyes glint in his shadowed face. "The fault is mine. I should not have frightened her. But I have seen such things..." His voice dwindled away until she could barely hear him. "And done such things..."

She knew he must have done terrible things, slaughtered people cruelly, destroyed cities. Such was the way of war. Her father's grandfather had fought bloody battles to drive the Seljuk Turks out of Armenia, and her own castle had passed though many previous families by way of arrow, sword and siege since its first stone towers had been raised. The Mongols were more successful at warfare than any since, perhaps, the great Alexander, but they would not be the last.

As for women and war... Her mind leapt to a vision of naked, terrified harem girls fleeing from Mongol invaders. From one tall, deep-voiced Mongol warrior in particular. If his face could blaze with fury, how might it blaze with lust? She looked away, hoping the twilight hid the flush of arousal mixed with shame on her own face, then turned quickly back. He must not think that she was repulsed.

"If you wish to speak of this, I am not so easily frightened, nor so ignorant." Whatever he had seen or done—she did not think it was a matter of rape alone—had scarred him. She would not add to his pain. When he remained silent she longed to touch him, for comfort, but instead gave a low whistle that brought her horse to the gate.

"You must meet Bakhshi," she said softly, and only then lay her hand briefly on Yul Darugha's arm to show the horse that she trusted this man.

The beautiful bay head lowered to take in the newcomer's scent then allowed itself to be stroked and scratched by him in all the right places.

Ardzvik, her shoulder brushing her companion's, breathed in his scent as well, of horse, leather and sweat, and some indefinable element that was his alone. She felt some of his tension recede. Here in the twilight, with their shared love of horses, it was as though they had always known each other.

At last he did speak, continuing to stroke the horse's glossy neck. "It is an old memory, raised anew when I saw you and your sister side by side in the town square. I have seen others with such golden hair from time to time, but there is one I cannot forget; scarcely more than a child, in the Sultan's harem, naked, shrinking into a corner in terror of my men, of me. Such a look on so beautiful a face." He retreated silently into his own thoughts for a moment, then went on. "Another naked girl, fair skinned with dark hair, faced us in a passion of rage, seeking to defend the younger. She wielded the jagged shard of a great broken vase, but the threat of its sharp edges was as nothing beside her snarling face, as wild and fierce as a she-wolf's." He paused again.

"There is more to tell?" Ardzvik braced to hear the worst, but would not prod him further.

He drew a deep breath and let it out. "The men behind me cheered, seeing a battle worth enjoying, its outcome certain. Their blood was up, as was mine. But a voice I scarcely heard— my own voice—ordered them back, and when some tried to rush past I turned my sword on them. On my own men! One I killed. A friend. A bastard like myself who had risen in Batu Khan's service. A man who had fought beside me for half my life." His hand clenched in the horse's mane.

"And the girls?"

"They escaped us, but there were other bands of men sacking the palace. I doubt they survived." A pause, and then, so low she barely heard, "Yet I cannot forget. They come in my dreams."

A full moon hovered above the distant mountain range, leaving every vale and hollow still in darkness. Torches burned in the castle gardens, and one moved along the path they had taken, coming toward them. Ardzvik yielded to impulse and put her hand on his shoulder, but Leyli's voice rang out from above them, and then the Persian interpreter's.

"My lord, the men grow restive."

Leyli added with a giggle, "They have finished all the wine the steward would supply."

"It is best that I go now." Yul Darugha's voice was rough. He stepped back from Ardzvik's touch.

She watched as he joined the other two and saw by the

torchlight that he took Leyli's hand from the Persian's arm and offered his own as support along the steep path.

The next morning Ardzvik rose early after tortured dreams. Never had she needed the solace of the mountain and her falcon more. Bakhshi carried her with Zepyur tethered to her leather hawking glove along trails and then trackless reaches until his mistress was sure they could not be followed. She dismounted, slipped the hood from Zepyur's head and loosed the bird to the breeze.

Today, she had brought her bow in hope of flushing larger game than the falcon could hunt. Wild goats were often seen at this height, and even boar might come to root among the tubers of mountain flowers. She pulled off her leather glove and kept an arrow at the ready, but her mind was not focused as much on the outer world as on her inner one.

Why did she yearn so for a man who might well not want her, or, if he did, might value her title more than her body? And if he wanted golden-haired Leyli, how could Ardzvik bear it? Their father had not wed Leyli's mother, but he had acknowledged the child, and if Ardzvik bore no heir, one of Leyli's would be accepted as ruler of Aragatsotn. Illegitimacy was not such a barrier in the ancient traditions of this land.

It was the begetting of children that obsessed Ardzvik now, not the bearing of them. She wanted this one man and no other, foreigner, destroyer, conqueror though he might be. She had known a mare who would let no stallion mount her save the one of her own choice. The horse had broken out, gone to her chosen mate in spite of her owner's different plan, and their offspring had turned out to be the finest the herd had ever known. Perhaps bodies knew things that minds did not.

Ardzvik's mind might be preoccupied by her treacherous

body's needs, but her eyes caught the hitch in her falcon's flight, and her ears caught the changed sound of the bells on the bird's ankle. Suddenly Zepyur was not hunting, but fleeing. A great white falcon more than half again her size rose over the mountain's shoulder.

A falcon of the north! A female gyrfalcon! Not native here, but the royal family of Georgia had possessed one when Ardzvik was a child, and she had seen it hunt. It was clearly hunting now.

Zepyur twisted and dived, eluding her pursuer again and again, but the other gained ground each time. Ardzvik shouted and raised her bow. Something moved below on the mountainside, but she had no time to look. Zepyur dived again, opening space between herself and her pursuer, and Ardzvik's arrow sped sure and true—until another's arrow met it in flight, and both spun together toward the earth.

Ardzvik whistled for her bird and quickly donned the hawking glove. Another whistle, yet more piercing, came from somewhere below. Zepyur soared to her mistress and perched, quivering, on the thick leather gauntlet. The white intruder glided down past the man whose dun horse raced up the steep slope, to land on the arm of a second rider following more slowly.

Yul Darugha gave a roar in a language Ardzvik did not understand, though the words were clearly curses. She swiftly hooded Zepyur, stroked her feathers to calm her, and set her to perch on a rock in a sheltered hollow, tethered to a wiry shrub. Bakhshi grazed nearby, the sounds of his browsing familiar enough to reassure the falcon.

Ardzvik stripped off her glove and advanced toward the approaching man, another arrow at the ready. Her heart still pounded from her sudden terror for her falcon, but fear had transmuted into a glorious, intoxicating fury.

He leapt from his horse, bow in hand, and ran toward her, coming to a sudden stop as she raised her own weapon in warning.

"You…if you…when I saw that it was you…" His deep voice cracked. "If you had killed my gyrfalcon, with my falconer as witness…" He stopped for breath. "I would have had no choice! You know that!"

"I aimed between them to distract your bird," she retorted in a cold rage. "If she did not veer off, the next arrow would have found her heart. And if your arrow had killed my falcon…"

"I aimed between them as well," he said, his voice steadier now.

Ardzvik clung to her anger, reveled in it, allowed it to spark from ice into fire. "For the sake of my people, I surrendered my province, but this is my own land—here I will stand and fight!"

Yul Darugha's eyes lit with a flame that was not anger. He set down his bow and shouted a command to his falconer waiting below. The old man shook his head doubtfully but moved away with the gyrfalcon on his arm and was soon out of sight.

"So there is a she-wolf in you after all! When I first saw you I thought—I hoped—but I could not be sure."

"A she-wolf?" Ardzvik's laugh was scornful. "Look higher. My name means 'eagle' in the old tongue. I am Lady of Aragatsotn, and more. My mother's line is said to be of those warriors from the lands beyond the Black Sea called Amazons by the Greeks." True, only the oldest grandmothers said this, but Ardzvik still felt it to be true. "I will defend my own."

"I see in you that warrior girl who haunts my memory."

Yul spoke now not as the Mongol Darugha but as a man who needed no title between himself and the woman he desired. "It is she I dreamed of, before last night, and then it was you. The only prize worth winning."

The heat of Ardzvik's anger flowed effortlessly into arousal, but she did not forsake her proud stance. "How can you be so sure of me? Was she not naked, that warrior girl?"

He stepped forward; she stepped back. Her own hand drew the rough tunic over her head and loosed the drawstring of the men's trousers she wore for hunting. Her strong, slim body stood bared to the summer sun, and to his burning gaze.

Just as he reached for her, she stepped forward into his embrace, rejoicing in the rumble deep in his chest, and the arms far stronger than her own that raised her off her feet to crush her against him. His mouth pressed hard on hers then moved into the hollows of her neck and over her shoulders in a frenzy of hunger for her flesh. When he lifted her yet higher to taste her firm breasts, she gasped and cried out and forced his head and mouth ever harder against them.

At last, needing more, and yet more, Ardzvik scrabbled at the jerkin of overlapping leather disks that left his muscular arms bare but kept her from rubbing against his chest.

"Are you more shy of the sun than I?" she panted. In seconds, his clothing was heaped along with hers. They rolled together atop this pile or onto nearby tufts of harsh grass, scarcely noting the difference.

At first Ardzvik rode Yul, her long dark hair flailing across his body as she savored the exquisite joy of easing inch by inch onto his great length and breadth. Men were more like stallions than she had ever dreamed.

Then he growled low, lurched atop her and thrust deep and

hard. Her hips arched upward to take him in still deeper. Her passage gripped him, yet let him slide in its wetness just enough to drive her to a peak of intensity close to madness. Sounds burst from her that were not words, and from him as well, until all she could hear was her own voice rising in a cry of triumph, her body wrenched by joy.

But Yul, she saw, when she could focus on anything outside herself, was braced above her on stiffened arms, face twisted, jaw grimly set, the cords of his neck standing out like tree roots. "I must..." he forced out the words. "I would not get a bastard on you!" He struggled to lift his great weight from her, to withdraw.

"Then you had better wed me," Ardzvik cried. "I will have now what is mine." Need surged in her again. She dug her hands into his clenched buttocks, gripped him close, and tightened her inner walls about his hardness until he had no words at all, only rough groans accelerating into a mighty roar. That sound, and the hot, fierce flow of his seed, sent her into a second spasm of joy.

At last, Yul rolled aside. She lay beside him, both breathing in the sun-warmed air as though they could never get enough. "I too will have what is mine," he said at last. "But what of your priest?"

"Father Kristopor?" Ardzvik gave a short laugh. "I'll wager that one will already have ordered extra candles for the ceremony in the chapel." She lifted her head enough to rest it on his damp chest. "What of your shaman? And the ceremonies of your people?"

A low chuckle made his chest rise and fall. "Much simpler. We pledge to each other outdoors under the Blue Eternal Sky with respect for Mother Earth, and the shaman chants such ancient songs and burns such herbs as he thinks proper. Each has his own ways. Then there is feasting, but that must be the same the world over."

"Well then, we have made good progress already under the Blue Eternal Sky. But more would surely not be wasted."

There was time, now, for Ardzvik to lean over Yul and explore his long, strong body, tracing the contours of his wide shoulders with her fingers, pressing her mouth into the hollow of his throat and feeling the vibrations of a moan too low for ears to hear. She moved her lips across his great chest and around his nipples. She licked at salty traces of sweat all the way down past his belly to where his skin became paler and more tender. By then the sounds of his pleasure were loud enough to signal renewed arousal, already clear from the rising of his shaft. Still he remained unmoving, letting Ardzvik enjoy her journey.

The temptation to take him into her mouth was great, but she moved past with only a teasing flick of her tongue at the dewy pearl on his tip. His hands tightened painfully on her arms. She kept on downward along his strong thighs, heavily muscled as only those of a man who'd spent his life on horseback could be.

"Let me..." Ardzvik twisted so that she knelt between Yul's widespread legs, gripping those powerful thighs and bending at last to savor the taste and feel of his hard, jutting shaft.

His hips rose to thrust himself deeper into her mouth. She matched his rhythm, hearing the harsh sounds tearing from his throat, feeling them vibrate into her own core as though he touched her between her legs—and suddenly she needed him there more than she needed breath.

She lifted her head. "Ride me!" she pleaded, rolling onto

her back, and at once Yul was on her, in her, his thighs gripping her flanks.

They raced together, soared together, until both shouted their triumph in tones as keen as any fierce pair of mating falcons. The sun, when they came to earth, was warm on their naked skin, and even clouds would not have diminished the inner heat they shared.

The horse grew restive. The falcon, knowing there was meat for her in the saddlebag, began to make her hunger known.

They could wait. Life would seldom be easy, peace was always fleeting, but nothing that bound together in joy the Lady of Aragatsotn and Yul Darugha would ever be a waste.

To Love a King's Man

Emma Jay

Inverness, Scotland, 1589 AD

Evanna stood on the stone stairs of the keep as her brother Alex swung open the wooden doors to welcome his friend Conal. She watched the men embrace and felt a pinch in her chest. There were no finer specimens of manhood in the Highlands.

Guests gathered at Armitage Keep for the annual Highland games, an event that caused great excitement throughout the region. Evanna had missed them the past three years because her husband had been in ill health and claimed the journey was too hard.

Since his death, she lived in her brother's home, serving as his chatelaine until he found another husband for her. As hostess, she doubted she'd have time to enjoy the games as she had when she was younger. The idea put her out of sorts.

Conal drew back from her brother's embrace and looked up the stairs, his blue eyes bright with humor.

Evanna battled to hide the delight welling inside her. He couldn't know she'd loved him since she was a girl, when he and Alex had run wild in the village, the laird's son and his best friend, a knight's bastard.

"Little sister!" Conal's voice boomed off the stone walls. "So glad you're home." He took the stairs two at a time and caught her in his arms.

She allowed him to hold her, long enough to memorize the impression of his hard body against hers, his earthy, horsey scent, before she pushed him away. He took an exaggerated stumble backward and grinned. She scoffed to hide the flush creeping up her cheeks at the impure thoughts filling her head. She'd been a maid when last she'd seen him, but now she'd been married. While her husband had been old and frail, she was aware of what could be between a man and a woman. Especially a virile man and his woman.

"Go on with you. You're smelling up my home."

"I'll just bathe in the horse trough."

"Don't you dare!" she exclaimed. "We have guests."

He leaned against the wall. "I am a guest."

She opened her mouth on a derisive sound, but cut it short when he arched a dark eyebrow. Her mouth closed with a click of teeth as she stared. He was a guest now, not simply a childhood friend. Even though he would forever be a knight's bastard, he'd proven himself in battle, winning the king's approval. The king had gifted him with a small keep to the north. So he was her guest...and tradition dictated that the chatelaine welcome guests with a bath.

A bath. Her hands on his body. She'd done the chore dozens of times but never had her skin tingled in anticipation.

She turned halfway up the stairs, pushing away thoughts of

a naked Conal, forcing herself to picture instead the sleeping arrangements of her other guests, and where she might put Conal.

The only room available was next to her own, the one she'd purposely left empty because she'd wanted a quiet escape, not a loud, raucous Highlander in the next room, belching and who knew what else.

Now Conal would sleep there, and she would get no sleep at all.

Conal hadn't been to Armitage Keep since he'd left for war. He walked to the window of the tower room Evanna had given him and looked down at the village. His mother had lived on the edge of town, marked a whore after she became pregnant with him.

Marked a whore, but not one. No man besides his father had a part in his mother's life when he'd been growing up. She'd died when he'd been on the continent, alone here in the town. He'd wanted her to move to his keep, the one the king had awarded him. She'd wanted to remain in the town she'd known, where she'd grown up, where she'd raised him to be a man whose name the king knew.

A knock on the door startled him. He turned to see a copper tub edging into the room, borne by two strapping lads, followed by three maids, all lugging steaming pots of water. The boys set the tub by the fire, and the young women filled it, watching him through their lashes. All but one, who met his gaze straight on. He wondered if she'd be the one to bathe him.

His loins stirred at the thought. She was a pretty thing, and bold. He liked a bold woman in bed. He opened his mouth to send the others off when the door opened and Evanna stepped in, a towel draped over her arm, a basket in her hand.

When last he'd seen her, she'd been all legs and arms, so scrawny a good wind could blow her away, her hair wild down her back. She'd run after his horse the day he'd left, tears streaming down her cheeks. Now she was a woman grown, her expression serene, her hair confined in a net at the back of her head, a net he suddenly wanted to toss away. He blamed the errant thought on his earlier arousal. She was his hostess and the sister of his best friend.

His gaze drifted over Evanna's simple dress, the soft fabric following the lines of her body, curving over her full breasts, hugging her trim waist. The shape of her body was imprinted on him since he'd held her against him on the stairs.

She dismissed the servants with a word, and they were alone, the only sounds the crackling of the fire and his pulse beating in his ears.

Impossible, since all his blood now pooled between his legs.

She set the basket on the chair by the fire. Soap and other supplies peeked out. "You don't mean to bathe me."

"It's my duty."

"Evanna, it's not... I'm bastard born."

"And a champion to the king. I'm honored to do it."

He blew out a laugh. "It is...odd." She'd been just a girl, and now she was his hostess.

"But not distasteful, I hope."

The baldness of her words shocked him into stillness.

"You won't be the first man I've bathed. I am a widow."

He'd known her husband, the old lecherous bastard, about the size of one of Conal's arms, and with half the number of Conal's teeth. Conal doubted the old man had shown his young wife the pleasures that could be had between a man and a woman.

The pleasures Conal wanted to show her. If he took off his clothes in his current state, his intentions would be clear.

How would she react? The way she watched him now, he couldn't be sure.

"The water is cooling." She folded the towel in front of her expectantly.

Perhaps a cold bath was the better choice. "I can bathe myself. I do it often."

She lifted her chin. "Conal."

"Evanna." Even in the privacy of his bedchamber, he knew he shouldn't be calling her by her given name. He stepped forward to take the towel from her. "I'm sure you have other duties."

"I wish to do it."

The words were soft, but strong, and she met his gaze. She wished to do it. She was a widow, and the way she looked upon him...

He eased away and stripped the linen shirt over his head, thinking she would change her mind when he met her challenge. She would scurry off and he would bathe in peace. Instead, she held her ground, her gaze lowering to his chest, her eyes darkening, her lips parting.

His balls tightened. He knew that look of arousal on a woman's face. He hesitated with his hand on his belt. If he removed his plaid, she'd see him in all his aroused glory, because God help him if he could control it right now. Her gaze dropped to his hands on his belt as if willing him to act.

"You might turn your back," he chided.

Her cheeks flamed and she pivoted with a swirl of skirts. He unfastened his belt and placed it on the bed, removing his plaid and folding the length of it, holding it against his cock lest she try to get a peek. He placed the plaid on the bed, removed his boots and stepped into the water, his back to her. Only when he was safely submerged, a washcloth floating over the most errant part of him, did he speak.

"You may turn around," he said, his voice rough.

She did, briskly, fetching her basket.

Evanna spent a moment fighting for control of her breath. The sight of Conal shirtless, his shoulders broad and sun browned, his chest dusted with a fine layer of hair, had left her dizzy. She'd seen warriors before, but none so fine and strong. And she'd volunteered to touch all that fine, strong skin. Already her fingers curled with anticipation.

Unable to meet his gaze lest he see her excitement, she took her place at the tub near his head.

"Lean your head back." She lifted a small pitcher from the basket and dipped it into the tub. He flinched when her hand touched the surface of the water, and he grasped at the washcloth that floated free, preserving his modesty.

She pressed her hand lightly to the warm skin of his forehead, urging his head back so she could let the water flow through his thick, short hair. She tunneled paths for the water with her fingers. His scent filled her nostrils, male and musky. She breathed it in, then reached for her soap, lathering it between her hands before sinking her fingers into his hair. He made a soft sound of pleasure and rested his head against the edge of the tub. She massaged his scalp, studying his face as she did so—the fullness of his lips, the straightness of his nose, the way his long, thick eyelashes rested against tan skin.

"I could shave you as well." She stroked a soapy hand along his jaw.

He opened his eyes to look into hers. "You will not."

She smiled, relaxing a little. This was Conal. A friend. "Do you not trust me with a razor?"

He chuckled, but didn't respond. Instead of liberating the washcloth he held so securely against his male parts, she used her hands to coast soap over his shoulders, enjoying the intimacy of skin against skin, pausing for a moment at a ridge of scar tissue just below his left shoulder.

"What is this?"

"A sword injury. Something too common in battle." His voice was tight.

"Yet you won't allow me near you with a razor," she teased, and he relaxed again.

She glided her hand down his chest, circling over his skin, mesmerized by the way the lather caught in the hair there. His breathing grew heavy, gusting against her cheek as she washed his flat stomach, following the line of hair below the water and—

He clamped his fingers around her wrist and lifted her hand from his skin.

She turned her head to see his nostrils flared, his eyes dark.

"That's all, Evanna. Go now."

She didn't want to go. She wanted to stay, to reach, to stroke. Her entire body was hot, tingling, aware as she'd never been. Even his calloused hand on her wrist sent shivers of delight up her spine.

"Conal, I—" But she didn't know how to tell him what she wanted. She looked into his eyes, which had gone flat.

And she fled.

* * *

Cursing herself for a coward, Evanna stood on the hill over-looking the hammer toss event. Her brother Alex lifted the heavy tool over his head, muscles bunching, and swung the hammer three times before letting it fly to land on the empty field. Cheers rose from the crowd. He lifted his hands in triumph, then turned to clap hands with a bare-chested High-lander wearing naught but his plaid.

Conal.

Her breath caught as Conal hefted a hammer to the line as if it weighed no more than a stick. Everyone stepped back as he raised the tool over his head and spun it in three tight circles, every muscle in his chest and arms defined with the effort.

He released the hammer and turned to watch its progress. Only after the crowd bellowed did she tear her gaze from him and see that his hammer had surpassed Alex's.

The two men bumped shoulders good-naturedly, then Conal reached for his linen shirt. As he pulled it on, he straightened and met Evanna's gaze, just as her housekeeper approached with questions about the night's feasts. Reluctantly, Evanna turned to attend to her duties.

That night she sat in the hall, on the dais, and watched the revelry of the athletes, the challenges shouted from one table to another, the raucous laughter. She couldn't tear her attention from Conal, who sat with her brother, receiving special atten-tion from the serving girls.

Evanna's stomach tightened, and she pushed her plate away, the food barely touched. All she could think of was how hard and warm his skin had felt beneath her hands, the crispness of his chest hair and how she wanted to feel him again, this time against her body, skin to skin. He'd rejected her once—would he reject her again?

Evanna stood outside Conal's bedchamber, shifting her weight as she worked up her nerve. She might not have another chance. The games were ending tomorrow. Conal would go his own way, and she would marry. She must act now.

Glancing over her shoulder to ensure no one was coming, she knocked, and hoped he was alone.

The door swung open with more force than she expected. Conal filled it, bare chested.

He scowled. "What do you want?"

"You," she murmured, and stepped into the room, curving her hand around the back of his head and pressing her mouth to his.

He tasted delicious, sweet from the wine, hot, masculine... She darted her tongue across his lips to take in the flavor of him. She was vaguely aware of him closing the door, more urgently aware that he wasn't returning her kiss.

She drew back and looked into his eyes. "Am I doing something wrong?"

His frown deepened. "You are too good for me, Evanna. God help me, I've dreamed about this, but there's no hope for a laird's daughter and a bastard."

She loosened the ties of her dressing gown. "Tonight, there is."

The fabric slid down her shoulders to pool on the floor. She stood naked and vulnerable for a moment before he swept her into his arms and covered her mouth with his.

Yes. He hadn't turned her away, and his kiss was everything her dreams had promised, commanding but warm. She wound her arms around him, pressing her cool flesh into his heat, savoring the rasp of chest hair against her breasts, his hair beneath her palms.

He angled his head, his tongue parting her lips, delving between with slow, sensual strokes that sent tingles along her skin. His rough hands coursed up and down her back, fingertips caressing her spine, bringing her closer.

Her sex pulsed with anticipation, an arousal she'd never experienced. Between them, his cock grew hard, prodding her belly. She glided her fingers down his waist, over the hard muscles of his stomach, to rest on his belt, but she couldn't work up the courage to unbuckle it.

He took the decision from her and reached between them to loosen it, letting the plaid and leather fall in one heap to the stone floor. Before she could reach for him, he took her hand and led her to the chair by the fire. He was perfection in male form, from his fine face to his broad shoulders marred by the sword injury, the broad chest, the flat stomach, and, heavens, a hard thick cock jutting out from a nest of dark hair. Just looking at him, imagining him filling her, pumping into her, made her sex grow damp.

"Come here," he urged, his voice rough, and guided her to straddle his broad thighs so her knees rested on the chair on either side of his hips.

He curved his hands around her hips, easing her closer. The heat of his cock was against her sex, taunting, not touching. Then, with an ease that belied the earlier hunger of his kiss, he glided his fingertips up her waist to caress her breasts, circling them lazily, plucking at her nipples until they hardened painfully, until she rocked her hips forward against his erection. He chuckled and shifted forward. He cupped his hand around the back of her head and drew her close for another kiss. She rocked forward again, reaching for him, wanting him as wild as he made her.

Capturing her wrists, he brought them to the small of her back, holding them captive in one big hand, and trailed his lips down the line of her throat, tasting her skin with tiny flicks of his tongue. He continued down the slope of her breast, until he reached her nipple. She held his gaze as he flicked it with his tongue and circled it, before closing his mouth on it and drawing deeply.

She moaned wantonly and let her head fall back, her hair loose down her back adding another sensation as it pooled against his thighs and her buttocks. He tightened his hand on her waist and suckled on her nipple, feeding his hunger, heightening her own. The petals of flesh between her legs grew slicker, and she bumped her mons against his cock, wanting more contact, needing release.

He chuckled against her skin and released her hands to free his own, which he dragged up the inside of her thigh to part her sex, stroking the little bundle of flesh atop her folds, lightly teasing. She groaned in frustration when he removed his touch from the swollen nub, and then in pleasure when he pushed two thick fingers inside her, pumping gently, hooking to caress her channel in ways she hadn't imagined. Her cream coated his fingers, and with each thrust, he pushed deeper.

"You're ready for me," he murmured wonderingly.

"Please, Conal," she murmured mindlessly, thrusting against his fingers, seeking fulfillment. "Please."

He removed his fingers and brought them to his mouth, sucking her juices from them, holding her gaze as he did so. Something quivered low in her belly. She'd never seen such a thing.

Then he used those same fingers to close around his cock, and urged her forward with his other hand. "Mount me, sweetheart."

She knew how to do this. Because her husband hadn't much stamina, he'd preferred her to ride him, but never had she been so eager as she rose up, parting her legs, and lowered herself onto Conal's cock.

The blunt head of him stretched her more than his fingers had, and she hesitated. He caught his breath and bumped his hips against her, sliding deeper. She relaxed her muscles and took him, pleasure and pain mingling as her body adjusted to his size.

He curved one hand over her bottom and with his other teased her breast, the tugs on her nipple sending twinges of delight to her womb, until nothing was in her head but the need for pleasure, and she began to move.

She pumped, watching the way he disappeared inside her, the hair of his groin tangling with hers. He cupped her head in his hand and kissed her as she rode him, his thumbs moving in circles high on her thighs, sending spikes of pleasure to the center of nerves above where they joined. She had never experienced such a desire, and wanted to press his hand to her sex and make him ease the building pressure. With each thrust she rolled forward, needing release.

He took pity and pressed his thumb to the tiny bundle of nerves, letting it ride there, so that with each thrust, her entire being focused on the pleasure between her legs.

Then, with one upward sweep of his thumb, he sent her into a maelstrom of sensation, her blood on fire, her skin sparking, everything hot and bright. She clung to his shoulders as she rode out the climax. He scooped her against him, lowering her to the rug before the fire, driving his cock deep, his skin slapping hers, her body clutching him, the slick sounds and moans of pleasure filling the room before he stilled, flush against her, then yanked out, his seed pulsing hot over her hip.

He rolled onto his back with a groan, one arm crooked over his eyes, and pulled her against him. After a moment, he turned his head to her, eyes glinting. "Next, we'll use the bed."

Evanna nestled against Conal's side and ran her palm across his chest as dawn filtered in through the window above the bed. She should be up, seeing to the duties of the day, but couldn't pull herself away. A strange sorrow filled her chest. Being in his arms was everything she could have dreamed, but now she must leave. Would they be able to find privacy before he left the keep, or was this the last time he would touch her, the last time she'd know his kiss?

He made a sound of contentment and shifted toward her, pulling her close. He kissed her lightly and smoothed her hair back from her face. "You should not have come here."

His words stung, and she drew free of his touch. "I heard no protest last night."

His brow furrowed. "You take my meaning. This between us—there can be nothing more. The difference in our stations is too great."

"Does that make what we felt less real?"

"Only more painful." He curved his hand over her cheek and forced her to meet his gaze. "I have loved you since I was a boy, Evanna. The memory of your face brought me through many battles."

Her breath caught in her throat and her entire being narrowed onto him, onto the words she'd longed to hear.

Then he continued. "But I cannot give you the station you deserve."

"I had that station once. I don't want it again."

"Your brother will feel differently. You must go to a husband who is your equal. It is your right."

She shifted on the bed, leaning into him, wanting to remember always the feeling of his body along hers. "My right should be to love whom I choose."

His eyes were sad as he stroked his thumb over the curve of her cheek and bent to kiss her, just as the door crashed open.

"Do you mean to be a lay-a-bed—what in hell?" Alex demanded when he spotted Evanna. "My sister? You dishonor my sister in my home?"

"Alex, no, I came to him." Evanna wrapped the sheet around her nakedness and leaped from the bed when Alex reached to drag Conal from it. "I came to him. I love him."

"Love him," Alex scoffed. "You cannot know him."

"I know him." She placed her hand on her brother's arm, wondering why Conal remained silent. Why did he not declare his love for her as he'd done moments ago?

Alex pulled free of Evanna's touch and turned to Conal. "We meet on the field in one hour."

A duel? Fear fluttered in her stomach. She could not lose either of them.

"You wish everyone to know Evanna spent the night in my bed?" Conal asked quietly. "You wish to expose her dishonor to your guests?"

Alex snapped his teeth together in frustration. "Fine. The caber toss. If I win, you leave and never return to Armitage Keep."

"Alex, no!" She couldn't drive this wedge between the men

who had been friends from the time they could walk.

"Fine," Conal said sharply. "But if I win, I wish permission to court your sister."

"Court her! She is a laird's daughter and you are a bastard!"

Conal winced at the use of the word from his friend. "I am the king's champion."

Alex narrowed his eyes. "One hour," he said, and spun out of the room.

Evanna stood at the edge of the field, forcing herself not to twist her hands as Conal hefted the tree trunk as tall as three men, and as heavy. He braced the caber against his right shoulder and worked his hands beneath to lift. She held her breath as he took several running steps, then heaved the caber away with enough force to make it flip so the top landed away from him. But the pole landed crookedly, not a perfect toss.

Her nails dug into her palms as he met her gaze across the field, his expression unreadable.

He crossed to right the caber, and held it steady while Alex bent to lift it. Her stomach tightened at the tension between the men. Conal stepped back and let Alex make his run. The caber left Alex's hands, flipping midair to land perfectly straight in the middle of the field.

Conal lost. Her knees wobbled. Conal's expression was bleak when Alex turned toward him, triumphant.

"A request of the champion!" Evanna called, her voice wavering. "I have a request to make of my brother."

Alex turned, his expression forbidding, so like their father she nearly lost her nerve. But she didn't waver. Instead, she walked to Conal's side. She didn't touch him, but stepped in front of him, facing her brother.

"I wish to marry for love." Her voice was not as strident as she hoped, but not as shaky as she feared. "Once, I married for family, for land. This time, I wish to marry for love, to a good man, a man you've called brother. A man I wish to call husband."

Alex looked from her to Conal, who placed his hand on her shoulder and eased up to her side. Alex's jaw tightened, and he turned away. Evanna's heart sank. She looked at Conal, who squeezed her shoulder, then released it.

"You would be happy in a small keep in the north, with a husband who is away more than he is home?" Alex demanded.

His words stole her breath, spread hope through her. She had thought about how difficult and lonely life might be while Conal did the king's bidding. But being alone for months was better than a life without him. "I would."

"And you," he barked to Conal. "You would be happy with my sister? You know what a pest she can be, stubborn and bossy."

Conal slipped his hand around her waist. "I will."

"Then, I suppose, if you can stomach her, I no longer have to."

Alex's growl was softened by a brief grin of apology. Joy flowed through her as she understood. He'd done his duty by challenging Conal, and now he'd set them both free. Because Conal was his friend? Because he loved his sister? She didn't take time to understand his reasons. Instead, she turned into the arms of the man she loved and kissed him for the world to see.

The Bodyguard

Jacqueline Brocker

Tajima Province, Japan, 1555 AD

Misato, Sen and Saitou walked through the marketplace that lay just beyond the palace grounds. Father had been reluctant to let Misato go, but she pointed out that it would be better to show that he, as *daimyo* Lord Yamana, wasn't protecting his daughter as though she were a fragile egg. Father, despite his seriousness, had laughed.

She didn't wish to buy anything; she just needed the walk outside the palace grounds. Her companion, Sen, was by her side, and Saitou strode just behind. Her bodyguard wasn't fully armored, but he wore both swords—his long *katana* and short *wakizashi*. He appeared relaxed, almost tranquil, but there was the bemused, though not unkind, glint in his eye that he often had.

Misato preferred that look to the one he'd worn when he'd first arrived.

Saitou's entrance into Father's palace had been both humble

and dramatic. He'd not wished to draw attention to himself, but he'd appeared disheveled and dusty in the palace court-yard where Misato had been practicing with her *naginata* instructor.

Saitou carried his helmet under his arm. Half of it was shat-tered. Black ash had smeared the right side of his face. More than that, his right earlobe was gone, a scab formed in its place. Yet under the grime was a slender, melancholy face, full of the humility and honor befitting a proper samurai.

Misato and her instructor lowered their practice weapons. The *naginata,* a long wooden shaft with a curved blade, was the favored weapon samurai women learned to use in case they had to defend their homes. Misato had always been competent at its use, but since the ninja first threatened, she had practiced with even greater vigor. The ninja's sudden appearance had kept her awake for a week.

Saitou had been taken to meet Father. Misato had excused herself from practice. She knew Father would want her in a meeting—a woman she might be, but she was his only child and close to coming of age. Sen dressed her in an appropriate *yukata,* and she'd entered Father's reception room in time to hear everything.

The samurai announced his name, and told her father he was once of Lord Kikuchi's palace in the neighboring Inaba province. Lord Kikuchi had been a great friend of Father's. But now Lord Kikuchi was dead, and the palace laid waste by siege. Those loyal to Lord Kikuchi had fought fiercely, but the Okubo clan had muskets.

Misato shuddered. She remembered hearing about these from her tutors, the long weapons out of which a tiny ball exploded with fire and smoke, penetrating its target with burning force. The shattered helmet, and the cause of Saitou's missing earlobe, were explained…an inch or so difference and Saitou might not have lived.

With a low, unhalting voice, Saitou told her father that he had stood by as Lord Kikuchi committed seppuku, cutting his stomach, and that once the act was done, Saitou beheaded him. An act of mercy after an honorable deed.

But before Lord Kikuchi died, as the siege reigned around them, he'd written a letter for Saitou to bring to her father, Lord Yamana. Saitou had walked for days to bear this message.

Misato tried not to look at Saitou with pity. For she knew that Saitou must have felt a weight of something akin to shame; many samurai in his position would have committed seppuku alongside their Lord. But having been instructed otherwise, he could not.

Father read the letter aloud. It contained much useful information about the Okubo's strategic matters, a suggestion that he might have to learn how to use the European weapons. And it also requested that Father, as a *daimyo,* accept Saitou's fealty.

Misato knew Father was honor bound to do so. Nonetheless she was pleased when he did. She was most surprised though by his first condition: he wanted Saitou to act as her bodyguard until they found the ninja that had attempted to take her life.

Saitou's face had been unreadable. It wasn't a position of great prestige, but Saitou wasn't of the highest class of samurai, so it wasn't inappropriate.

When Saitou said he would be greatly honored to do so, Misato's chest tightened.

He was given a room near hers and given instructions about the layout of the palace. He was to be with her constantly. Misato wanted more than anything for the ninja to be caught.

Yet while they waited for him to move, Saitou's presence was... very welcomed.

Some of the other samurai with fealty to Father found Misato amusing with her interest in Father's role and her determination to master the *naginata*. But despite Saitou's bemused expressions, he didn't talk to her as if she were a fool. Instead of teasing her every day once her *naginata* practice was finished, he'd say he'd not want to meet her in battle, and he meant it.

At least, Misato hoped he did.

At the end of the market stood a small waterway, and over it a bridge that led into the town, and beyond that sat the rice fields. Misato, Sen and Saitou reached the base. Misato made to step onto the bridge when Saitou spoke.

"We cannot go into town, my lady. It is too far from the palace."

"But I would like to stand at the top of the bridge for the view." She met Saitou's gaze, offering a challenge. "If that is not too much to ask."

Saitou gave a little bow. "That is acceptable."

The three of them reached the rise of the bridge. Around them people wheeled carts, children hurried about in their games and there was a general chatter in the air. Misato smiled. Everywhere was full of life.

Sen waved. Misato looked up to see some other women of Sen's age gathered together on low seats on the town side of the bridge. Sen glanced at Misato with a soft pleading, but then turned away.

"Go," Misato said. "Saitou will stay with me."

Sen bowed, thanking her, and hurried down the bridge to see her friends.

"That was kind of you," Saitou said softly.

Misato sighed. "Is it a kindness if you do so because you wish to be alone? Sen is with me day and night, and she is a good servant, but sometimes…"

"I'm still here," he said, nothing in his tone to tell her how he felt about that.

"Ah, but I can't dismiss you so easily." *Nor do I want to*, she thought.

Saitou grinned his almost imperceptible grin. "No, you cannot."

They stood in silence for a while. And then Misato asked, "How do you find Tajima province after Inaba?"

"It is…noisier. I like the quiet myself. But it is more than acceptable."

She nearly gave an unfeminine grunt. His answer revealed nothing. "Were Lord Kikuchi's lands quiet?"

"Sometimes, yes. We were near the sea. I could almost always hear it at night." His face became dreamy, a little melancholy. "I do miss that sound here."

Misato swallowed. "I'm sorry."

Saitou closed his eyes and shook his head as if to rid himself of the memories. "I did my duty to Lord Kikuchi. That is what matters. As I will do my duty to Lord Yamana."

"And to me?" she asked, tilting her head.

Saitou once more smiled. "Of course." He gazed out over the river. "I wonder why someone wants you dead. It seems an unnecessary way of getting to Lord Yamana."

He wasn't asking her opinion, but she gave it anyway. "Hardly. Father is currently aligned with the Fujiwara clan, but the Sanjos would like him to side with them. My thinking is that without my mother, my father has only me. He stubbornly refuses to remarry, so I am very important to him. The Sanjos could have me killed and blame the Fujiwaras. If father believes them, he might do something rash, ending ties with the Fujiwaras."

Saitou looked at her, surprised. "You've given this a lot of thought."

"Every night since the ninja came," she said, her voice flat.

Saitou glanced at her, his expression sympathetic. "You were awake the whole time."

Misato jerked, but then nodded. No one had guessed that.

It had been the soft swish on the balcony that had alerted her. No one in the palace would creep so carefully without reason, and no one should have been near her room. She knew exactly where her *naginata* stood, but she hadn't been able to move. Fear had paralyzed her.

Even when a shout stopped the intruder, and a thundering of running feet and cries followed by a deep splash in the moat, brought the whole incident to an end, she had not moved. She let Father believe she had slept through the whole incident, only wakening to the commotion. She didn't wish to worry him.

"I'm sorry you were frightened. But you can be assured, my lady; I will protect you."

His voice was so sincere Misato could only bow her thanks.

Saitou's gaze drifted to the river. Unfocused, melancholy, and a touch amused. Like life was both tragedy and comedy. Misato took in the planes of his face, the perfect styling of his hair, the smoothness of his forehead where it had been shaved back. Even with his missing earlobe, he was still a handsome man.

If he knew what she did at night when she couldn't sleep...

Abruptly, without looking at her, he asked, "Are you staring at my injury, my lady?"

She started. How did she explain it? After a moment, she

said, "I...was wondering if it still caused you pain."

"It's tender, but healing well." He touched it, self-conscious.

"Still, I shouldn't have stared."

Saitou turned and grinned. "Well, you were hardly gawping at my handsome face."

Misato's whole body froze, and she was locked in his gaze.

His grin faltered, and he swallowed.

Misato followed the rise and fall of his throat. Awkwardness hung between them like a monkey bent on mischief. At last, she forced a bright laugh. "Oh, you're funny, Saitou. Very funny!"

Either he took the hint, or he believed her false laugh, for he bowed, and said, deeply serious, "I serve my lady, to protect or entertain."

This time Misato's laugh was real, but it came to an abrupt halt. A man was approaching.

Even through her laugher, Misato heard the too-careful steps. She turned and saw him, his face covered in black cloth, thrusting a dagger toward her chest. She swayed in shock.

Saitou was faster than both. He drew his *wakizashi,* and leapt in front of Misato, blocking the strike with a swift sideways move. The dagger sliced the material of her kimono at the sleeve.

Saitou made to strike the man, but the ninja snatched his blade away and pushed Saitou so that he stumbled against Misato. Misato tumbled back, catching Saitou in her arms. His weight made them both fall onto the wooden planks of the bridge.

The ninja ran down the bridge and into the town, disappearing into the crowd. A small crowd rushed toward them, but Saitou was on his feet, running after the ninja.

Misato stood with the help of two women.

Sen came back, her face pale. "My lady!"

"I'm unhurt," Misato said, her voice calm despite the heartbeats hammering inside her chest.

A few minutes later, Saitou appeared again, his face sweaty and red, and his eyes enraged. "I couldn't catch him; he disappeared into the crowd." He looked at Misato. "You are safe?"

"Yes. Thanks to you." Misato gave him a look that was filled with more than gratitude.

If Saitou recognized what she meant, she couldn't tell, for he only bowed, and said they should return to the palace.

Two weeks later, Misato still could not sleep.

Sen, of course, slept soundly on her pallet.

Misato sighed. She eased herself out from under the light blankets, raised herself from the tatami floor, and slipped on her *yukata*. It was summer and the night was pleasantly warm. She lifted her *naginata* from the wall, pushed aside the paper screen that lead to the balcony, closing it softly behind her, and went on her now nightly walk.

It was perhaps a foolish way to relax, but it returned some of the sense of control that had been robbed from her when she first heard the ninja outside her door five weeks ago.

Misato kept alert, her eyes scanning the corridors of the palace, the pathways of the grounds. She made her footsteps as light as she could. She avoided the guards who, if they had found her, would have scolded her and escorted her back to her room.

She finished her usual route and returned toward her room along the balcony. Just before the entrance screen to hers was Saitou's room. Misato's body ran warm at the thought of him.

If she were honest with herself, her nightly walks now held another purpose.

On the first night, Misato had stopped, only glancing at the door, trying not to think of him in there, sleeping, his kimono undone, his hair in that natural disarray acquired from a night's rest.

She had been about to move on when she heard a soft moan from inside.

It was the sound she'd heard the soldiers making when they thought they were alone and no women were around to hear. The sound she sometimes made when she was alone, and Sen was fast asleep.

Saitou was pleasuring himself. His breathing was steady at first. But it became increasingly haggard, and she could even hear the rustle of material as his hand must have moved along the length of his shaft.

Misato had put her hand over her mouth, trying to contain the thought of what his shaft must have been like. She had caught some views of the woodblock prints that Father thought she did not know about. She had been taught how babies were made, and been informed it could be pleasurable for both parties, but it did not prepare her for the expressions of passion she had seen on those prints.

The tension of being caught and the delicate sensations coursing through her had paralyzed her on the first night. She'd wanted to run, but he soon reached his climax. It was only after, as he panted, that she stepped as quietly as she could away and into her room.

At first, she had only stood and listened with such attentiveness she could hear when he altered his technique, when his strokes became slower or faster. These nights, she knelt. Still gripping her *naginata,* she dove her hand beneath her clothing and with her finger sought out the tiny bud above her sex.

Virginity was something a samurai woman kept until marriage. Misato knew this pleasure would not rob her of that. Still, she was aware she crossed a line as she listened to his lusty noises and touched herself. It was like enacting an intimacy with him, her bodyguard, and a samurai not of highest rank. Not proper at all.

And her shame was for more than propriety. For each night, when he was done, he would weep. As much as his pleasure excited her, she wished more than anything to go to him, to comfort his tears. He must have been holding so much together during the day, being strong for both his former master, Father, and for her.

But she couldn't stop her hand from seeking out her sex.

Each time he climaxed quickly. She never made it with him, his speed too much for her. She always left unsatisfied, carefully moving back to her room. Still, she rolled and rubbed her hardening bud, the raised flesh smooth as a berry's skin. She sunk her teeth into her lower lip, keeping herself quiet.

Until her fingernail accidentally flicked the tenderest part of it, and she moaned.

She stopped moving, caught her breath. No sounds came from Saitou's room. She waited. Maybe he had heard nothing?

The screen flew open. Saitou clutched it, his nightclothes in disarray. When he saw Misato, his face filled with horror.

"What are you doing here?" he breathed.

Misato stood shakily. "I...I..."

He grasped her shoulders. "You should be in your room!"

His eyes were fierce. But Misato didn't care. Her body was too alight with desire for him.

"I'm sorry to have intruded. But..." She took a step forward, and pressed her hand against his groin. He was still hard, and his shaft beat against her hand. "Let me comfort you."

Saitou dropped his hands from her shoulders, his eyes widening. "My lady..." He took a step backward into his room.

Misato followed him, her hand not leaving him. "Let me. Please."

He shook his head. "No. I cannot let you. I'm your body-guard, your social inferior—"

Misato squeezed his shaft, and he sighed. "Let me," she said, making her voice gentle. "Let me give you the comfort you crave."

Saitou closed his eyes, and she saw the moment he gave in to his desire. He shut the screen behind her and caught her in his arms. As he kissed her, she dropped the *naginata*. She barely heard it land, for pulsing blood raced through her ears. Her body had been warm before, prickled with the heat of tension, and now it was flooded by fire.

They sank to the floor on their knees. Saitou continued to kiss her as she pulled apart his kimono and found what she was looking for. She drew back for a moment, holding him away so she could look. The moonlight shimmering in through the rice paper bathed his long, hard shaft. A delicate drop of his seed sat like a pearl on the head. The whole thing was like him, slender yet muscular.

Misato met his gaze and smiled, delight spreading through her, and took his sex in her hand.

"Oh my lady..." Saitou closed his eyes, his fingers flexing on her shoulder.

She moved her hand up and down the length, squeezing but

a little. She watched her gestures at first, amazed at how easily he fit to her, delighted at how she engulfed him and made him grow at her touch. "I am unpracticed; tell me what you need."

He nodded, his throat bobbing, and he guided her, asking her to grip him tighter or loosen her touch. She listened to him, changing her hand's motion and pressure until he gasped, "This! Just like this…" His voice was hoarse, and he leaned into her, pulling her closer, his lips at her cheek and ear.

She shut her eyes, pressed her cheek and chin into the crook of his neck, and sank into sensations–the musky scent of him, the warmth of his solid shaft, the strength of his embrace.

Saitou kept repeating under his breath, "*Yes, yes, yes… please, yes.*"

Misato smiled to herself, a little surge of triumph welling in her, knowing she had him under her command and with such a simple gesture. When he begged her to go faster, she slowed down, and only when he whimpered did she do as he asked.

He came all over her hand, with her panting in time with his labored breaths. When she drew back, his expression was hazy, yet utterly content.

Misato smiled and kissed him.

His glance speared her. "Now, let me return the favor."

Misato started. That was another matter. "I would like that, Saitou, but my virginity…"

He nodded, understanding. "You will still be a virgin. After all, if you can manage to stir yourself and still be one, I can too."

Heat blossomed in her cheek. "You saw?"

He winked at her in his wry way.

Still she asked, "Are you sure?"

He said nothing, only guided her shoulders to the floor.

With small defiance, she propped herself up on her elbows to watch as he pulled open her *yukata* and moved aside her underclothes. His fingers brushed along her skin as he did, and she twitched at the feeling, the touch of a man so foreign to her, but completely pleasurable.

Her wet sex soon lay exposed to the air of the room. She bit her lip. If he slipped his fingers inside her, that might break her hymen, but what else was he planning?

Saitou gripped her hips with both hands, and guided her sex to his mouth.

Misato gasped. "Oh..."

His tongue was like a hot stone laid over her sex, hard and warm, yet oddly flexible. That was unusual, the feeling of something else dexterous and thick sliding along her folds. He found her bud and pressed against it. Not as insistent as her finger—at first she barely felt its presence—but he continued to lick and probe, and it coaxed her bud to grow engorged. The rest of her body became still as stone. She couldn't move her limbs yet they hummed. Every part of her hummed.

One hand left her hip. Saitou grasped one breast and squeezed it.

Misato sighed. Even beneath the material, her nipple hardened toward his palm. He kneaded her breast, the movements both gentle and strong, and then his thumb found her nipple.

Misato, not thinking, arched into the touch. She clasped the back of his head, not forcing him closer, but wanting to feel the connection, to feel him between her legs and beneath her fingertips to increase their intimacy. She found herself rolling with his tongue, her hips acting without her instruction. She had no words for the sensations, and so only moaned softly, aware that they could not be heard.

This was so different from the pleasure she found with her own finger. By herself, she knew exactly what to do. Though there was much pleasure, there was little surprise.

Saitou, learning her, startled her, experimented in tender ways with her sex.

Her gaze cast down and met his. She half expected one of his teasing smiles to shine through his eyes, but all she saw was tenderness and desire for her.

Suddenly, he stopped. His tongue sat on her bud, but didn't move. Her sex pulsed, and frustration began to blossom in her belly.

Misato dug her fingers into his scalp. "Saitou, please—"

He closed his eyes and began again.

Words left her as he renewed his attention with great speed. She moaned, covering her mouth, unable to contain herself as the flick and roll of his tongue gave her new pulses of pleasure, each building on the last, moving faster and faster so she couldn't keep track of each sensation. It became a blur of pleasure, a constant reeling ecstasy that sent her body into a fever. As if her body was pushed to a point where everything might shatter.

And then she could no longer contain the pleasure. Her thighs began to tremble, then her stomach, her arms, until the burst came from between her legs and swept over her entire body. She cried out into her palm, turning this way and that, as if she could brace herself from the sharp, delicate, yet all-consuming sensations.

Saitou left his mouth on her, moving it while she came, until the storm subsided and left her feeling tender all over.

Her hand left her mouth. She cradled the back of Saitou's head.

He rose, leaned over her, and smiled.

She said, "That was…"

"I know. I could feel you." He winked at her, and chuckled. "You let yourself go so beautifully…" He trailed his fingers down her cheek, over her throat and across her collarbone. "Such ferocity when you train, such a sharp mind…and such passion for sex. You may well be the ideal woman."

"Not docility and perfect obedience?"

He chuckled. She cupped his cheeks. Her fingers accidentally found his injury. Saitou exhaled, and Misato leaned up to kiss it.

He sighed, a sound almost like weeping. "I would have gladly died alongside my Lord, but he wished otherwise. When I walked here, as sworn as I was to my master's promise, I desired nothing more than to die. Yet…you…"

Misato kissed him. She brought to the kiss not just her lust but her love, for she knew now that was what she had grown to feel for Saitou.

Saitou broke the kiss and shook his head. "Not that I can have—"

A sound whispered across the floor of the balcony.

Misato and Saitou both looked up, both remained completely still.

Outside, framed in the moonlight, was the ninja, moving down the balcony.

Saitou whispered, "He's going to your room. You're not there."

Misato nodded, until a feeling of horror ran through her. "But Sen is."

She swept up her *naginata* and flung herself out of the room. She ignored Saitou's voice as she took up a stance, *naginata* held above her head, heedless of her gaping robe. "Hey!"

The ninja turned. He didn't speak, but she could see in the space that revealed his eyes that he was smirking. That he believed she would be no match for him.

In his hand, a knife glinted in the moonlight.

Rage welled up in her, rage that he would dare take her life, that he might have killed gentle Sen, that he had caused her nights of distress, that he had been so bold as to try and take her life in the street.

Misato cried out and brought down the *naginata*.

But the ninja ducked, and rolled out of the way. Directly toward her. He leapt upright to his feet, mere inches from her.

Misato froze. Her long-range weapon was suddenly rendered useless.

The smile in his eyes was terrible.

She exhaled her last breath—

Suddenly, Misato fell to one side. She stumbled, and looked up. In her place Saitou stood in a lunged pose. He clutched his short sword, which was buried in the ninja's stomach.

Saitou twisted the sword.

Misato started as the ninja's body jerked.

With a swift motion, Saitou withdrew the sword and stepped back as the ninja fell to his knees.

Her would-be assassin slumped forward, head striking the wooden planks. He didn't move again.

Blood spilled from the ninja's body. Misato hurried to her feet, aided by Saitou, who closed her robe and then held her to him as they stared at the ninja. They breathed in time. Misato was hardly able to believe it was over.

Sen appeared at the open screen, bleary eyed, until she caught sight of the ninja's body. She screamed.

Misato went to her and took her in her arms, reassuring her quietly.

Sen's scream brought the guards, and eventually, Father. Misato and Saitou had no time to confer on the events, but they knew, instinctively, what their story was: that they had both heard him, both went to confront him, and before he could strike Misato, Saitou killed him.

Father glared at her. "You went to confront him? Misato!"

"I knew Saitou would wake soon. I'm not so foolish to think I could take on the ninja by myself."

She could tell, if perhaps no one else could, that Saitou was trying not to smirk.

Father sighed, shaking his head. "You're so willful sometimes. But I cannot be too angry, for you are alive." He turned to Saitou. "You have saved my daughter's life. I will bestow great honor on you for that. Tomorrow, we will speak. Please consider how I may do so."

Misato caught Saitou's gaze, making sure he understood exactly what to ask for.

The amused glint ran briefly, before he gave Father a serious, respectful bow.

Misato knew she had go to Father before he and Saitou spoke. She would be able to give him reasons why Saitou would be a good match that didn't involve the mention of love. It might take some convincing, but Saitou had saved her life twice. If Father wanted to hand her to someone who could protect her from further threats, he'd make no better choice. On the surface it would be an excellent match.

And beneath, Misato thought with hot anticipation, it would be tender and passionate, and loving.

BROKEN VOWS

Anya Richards

Lancashire, England, 1195 AD

T alk in the hall was subdued, for the lord was in poor spirits and it caused all to stifle the laughter they usually shared in the evening. Casting her husband a glance, Lady Mary de Charnesse took a sip of her wine. Sir Gareth was glaring at his trencher, his dark brows drawn together, the corner of his mouth sloping down.

Her heart sank. A cold shiver of fear trickled along her spine.

He is not Sir Guy, to fly into a rage.

Yet, even knowing her present husband was of far fairer temperament than her former, it took all her courage to lean toward him. "Is aught amiss, my lord?"

He jerked as though startled awake, and in a distant tone, said, "Nay, my lady. As is usual, the repast is delicious." As though to prove his words, he bore a bit of fowl to his mouth, effectively ending the exchange.

With a silent sigh Mary turned back to her own meal, but not before risking another glance at the handsome profile, the sweep of light-brown hair tied back and displaying a finely shaped head. Just that glimpse made her heart stumble and her breasts tingle.

There was nothing about Sir Gareth she found displeasing. Everything, from his muscular body—broad of shoulder and slim of hips, with the strong legs of a man used to long hours in the saddle—to his winning way of speaking to everyone, appealed.

Why have I been so cursed? First an old husband, foul-tempered with infirmity, and now a young, beautiful husband who cannot bear to look upon my face.

Tears pricked her eyes, but Mary kept her back straight and chin raised, only looking down to hide her dismay. There was no need to cry. With Sir Gareth at her side, the danger of losing her holdings to one of Sir Guy's perfidious nephews was past. And even though only three seasons had passed since his arrival, the land and its people thrived.

Sir Gareth was firm and just, winning the hearts of those he led, and the castle was once more a safe, peaceful place. Indeed, despite the strain of being tied to a man who clearly despised her, Mary knew herself blessed.

Alas, how much easier it would it be if he were ugly, within or without.

But Sir Gareth was neither, and each day Mary found herself drawn to him more—wanting to hear his booming laugh, feel the strength of his arm beneath her hand, be graced with a smile. Most of all, each night she dreamed of having him in her bed, the imaginings so bewitching she awoke heavy-eyed and sad at finding herself still alone.

He had made it plain from the first that he would not touch her. Having taken an oath before God, he'd promised never to lie with a woman again. When she'd asked him why he'd done it, he'd tersely said 'twas a matter of chivalry and nothing more.

To be denied her marriage bed because of chivalry! It made her want to howl.

Even inundated with disappointment, she was once more drawn to look at him.

He was staring at her, face stern and still, his darkening blue eyes making Mary's heart leap. Heat bloomed across her chest, rose to her cheeks, and although she wanted to turn away, his gaze held her captive as surely as if she were bound.

With a muttered curse he rose, pushing back his chair with enough force it teetered on its stout legs. The sound of it righting itself was like a thunderclap, made extraordinarily loud by the subdued atmosphere. There was a muffled scream in response, the sound of something falling to the floor. Without a word, Sir Gareth strode toward the door, leaving Mary stricken at this final evidence of his lack of regard.

Even worse were the expressions on the faces of their people. Fear, trepidation, sorrow. It harkened back to Sir Guy's last days, when none were safe from his ill temper. When none knew how their lord would react to a simple comment or commonplace occurrence. To imagine those days returning transformed her cold dread to heated anger.

Blackthorn would not return to those times.

She would not allow it.

Gareth strode through the tiltyard, his cock so hard it made each step a painful penance for his ill temper and arrogance.

Render unto Caesar what is Caesar's. He heard the earl's voice in his head—a mocking reminder of his assurance this insane plan would work. *I don't ask you to break your oath,* he'd said. *Simply to keep the one you swore to secure my holdings and stand with me as your liege. Lady Mary is plain and will offer no temptation. 'Twill be a simple matter of overseeing the lands, ensuring none encroach upon them.*

Entering the shadowy stables, Gareth ground his teeth to halt the string of foul curses rising in his throat. No doubt the earl believed what he said, but Gareth most certainly didn't agree. Lady Mary affected him in a way no other woman ever had. One look from her glorious brown eyes made him want to fall to his knees and beg for her favor, her heart, her body. One soft touch of her fingers had him cursing the youth and misplaced chivalry that had caused him to take a vow he now bitterly regretted.

In the desert, lonely and afraid, hearing that his first love Lizbet had wed another had caused frustration and self-pity to turn to pain. Time had eased the sting, and coming home to discover she had died birthing her husband's babe had only intensified the suspicion he'd been a fool. His folly had started when he'd left for Palestine with nothing except her whispered promise to wait for him, and it ended with a binding vow that threatened to ensure he would never know happiness at all.

Snatching up a saddle, Gareth threw it onto his charger's back and cinched it tight.

Each breath of Mary's subtle, lilac-tinged perfume, each glance, every smile drew him further under her spell. Just the memory of her cheeks turning pink beneath his perusal made him growl, ravenous for her.

Gareth swung onto Raven's back and kicked the horse into motion. He'd ride tonight until he'd whipped these crazed feelings back and locked them away.

Yet, he knew the best he could hope for was exhaustion—enough to allow him one night's sleep not haunted by imaginings of wrapping his wife in his arms, of burying himself inside her body, of holding her and never letting go.

By the time he returned, it was to find the castle's denizens already settled for the night, wrapped in blankets around the fireplace. Gareth could feel the stares as he crossed the hall, the weight of them only increasing his guilt. He'd thrown aside all noblesse oblige with his actions this eve, embarrassing Lady Mary and frightening their people.

According to the seneschal, Lady Mary's deceased husband had injured his leg, and his temper had festered along with the wound, leaving him crazed with pain, unpredictable and brutal before his death. Gareth's actions must have revived memories of that time. Ashamed, he vowed to do better, no matter his frustrations.

How many other fourth sons, without land or wealth, were as blessed as he? Being chosen to marry Lady Mary had been the greatest of honors. While the acreage was small, the land was fertile, productive and well positioned. No man who held it could consider himself unfortunate, and he needed to remember that rather than dwell on what he lacked.

Thus fortified, he pushed open the door to his room, stepping through and pausing at the sight of the old chamberlain nodding in a chair near the fire. It caused another stab of guilt, knowing he'd kept the man waiting to assist him with his bath.

Hearing the door, the chamberlain jumped to his feet,

apologizing and coming forward to help Gareth disrobe.

"Nay, John, find your pallet. I will tend to myself tonight."

But the man insisted on fussing about before he left and, as the door closed, Gareth rubbed his face, suddenly weary. Stripping off his clothes, he lowered himself into the water and sighed with pleasure. Blackthorn Castle truly was a most comfortable abode. How often in the desert had he dreamt of bathing, of not being coated in sand, and being able to use as much water as he pleased? Even the short tub, which caused his knees to stick up above the bathwater, was a joy and he slid down as far as he could.

The sound of the door opening caused a flash of annoyance, but he kept his voice low and even. "There is no need to watch over me, John. I told you to seek your rest."

"And he obeyed you, my lord, as any of your loyal servants would."

The sound of Mary's soft, light voice had Gareth's head jerking up, and instinctively he began to rise. Then he remembered he was unclothed and plopped back into the tub, causing a wave of water to slide over the edge. Reaching for a linen square, he hastily dropped it over his thickening erection.

"M...my lady..." Surprise and the sudden dryness of his mouth made him stutter.

Looking over his shoulder, seeing Mary coming toward him, he lost the ability to speak altogether. Her simple robe flowed loose but moved against her tall, slim frame, hinting at the enticing body beneath. Her dark hair was braided into one long plait, and in the flickering light her face was severe, mysterious, and reminiscent of paintings of the Madonna he'd seen on his travels.

Coming to stand beside the tub, she looked down at him,

her expression almost cold. His heart hammered with a sickening mix of fear and desire.

"I apologize for interrupting your leisure, my lord, but I seek your counsel."

Gareth swallowed, trying to marshal his thoughts and ignore the way his cock rose to full stand between his thighs. "I am at your mercy, my lady."

Mary blinked, as though surprised at his choice of words, and retorted, "As are all the people of Blackthorn at yours, my lord."

It would be cowardly to avoid her gaze, so he held it despite his shame. "I know this, my lady, and apologize for my surliness."

Mary sighed, as though with relief, and Gareth relaxed to see her eyes warming to their familiar gleaming brown.

"Thank you, my lord."

She suddenly knelt, the graceful motion bringing her face level with his and causing her scent to envelope him in a sweet, enticing cloud.

"Your presence has made a great difference to the spirits of those at Blackthorn. I would be distressed to see the amity you've achieved destroyed."

He couldn't let her praise him for the changes to the atmosphere of the keep. "Without your kindness and gentle care, your acceptance of me, I know the folk of Blackthorn would not be as well off as they are."

The beguiling wash of color flowing into her cheeks made his stomach clench, and the night seemed to close in, cloaking them in intimacy.

As though suddenly unsure, Mary looked down at her sleeve, which she rolled up to beyond her elbow. Gathering the trailing end, she knotted it, leaving her forearm bare. "I thank you for so saying."

She switched to her other sleeve, and it suddenly occurred to Gareth what she was doing—why she was doing it. The thought of her hands on his skin as she bathed him made him shiver.

"While my parents lived, Blackthorn was a happy place, and I'm pleased to see it return to the way it was." She reached for the soft soap.

He should stop her. Yet yearning kept him silent, stricken to stillness.

She drew her hand back, as though changing her mind, and Gareth expelled his pent breath, caught between relief and acute disappointment. He wasn't prepared when she deftly untied the thong holding his hair and pressed him forward. Unable to resist, he bent to allow her to pour water over his head.

"Sir Guy was proud and exacting," she said, her voice soft, "but also good to the people, an attentive husband until he was injured."

Sadness tinged her voice, and Gareth's muscles locked. The thought of Sir Guy touching Mary fomented a rising jealousy in his belly. He was glad she couldn't see his face, masked as it was by his hair, for his teeth were bared, and he knew she'd see the ire in his gaze. Clenching his hands into fists, he used the pain of his short nails digging into his palms as a distraction.

Almost as though sensing his rage, she fell silent. Soap ran over his head, and Gareth steeled himself. As Mary began to wash his hair, rubbing his scalp with strong, firm strokes, it was the most sublime of agonies. Each touch drove straight from his head to his groin, and it took every ounce of control not to groan aloud with the excruciating ache of overwhelming desire.

Regret and relief mingled inside him as she rinsed his head, and Gareth screwed his eyes closed to avoid getting the stinging liquid into them. After she was finished, he slicked his hair back and straightened. Wiping the lingering droplets from his face, he turned to look at his wife.

Her eyes were downcast, dark lashes hiding her thoughts, but the corners of her mouth were tight and her fingers clung, white-tipped, to the edge of the tub. Sadness lingered on her face, and Gareth wanted so badly to hold and reassure her, but he dared not move. If he touched her, he'd have to have her, and all would be lost, his immortal soul consigned to Hell.

Suddenly her eyelids rose, revealing the gleam of tears. "Please, my lord." Her voice was resolute but quavered under the strain of her emotions. "I know you didn't seek this marriage, but I beg you, do not let your mislike of me cause you to cast Blackthorn back into fearful times."

Stunned, Gareth could but stare, his mouth agape.

Before he found the wherewithal to reply, Mary rushed to continue. "Simply tell me what to do to make your being here more bearable."

The words tumbled one upon the other, and her voice cracked at the end, the impact of it like a lance striking Gareth's chest, causing the air to seize in his lungs for a moment. When he could once more move, he was unable to curtail his harsh bark of laughter.

Mary reared back as though slapped, all color fleeing her face, but she held her ground, keeping her back straight, her gaze trained on his.

Even with the anger and lust coursing through his veins, Gareth couldn't help admiring her courage. "Is that what you think, my lady? That my ill temper stems from some mislike of you?"

Each grated word made her eyes open wider, her expression one of confusion. "Aye...why else...?"

Without thought of what he was doing, with only his passionate fury and arousal holding sway, Gareth grabbed her hand and pulled it into the water, placing it over his aching erection. "This is why, my lady. This, and nothing else."

For a long moment Mary was unable to move, to breathe. Looking into Gareth's eyes was like gazing into a storm. The rigidity of the flesh beneath her hand seared her palm, the heat flashing up her arm into her breasts, her belly, the realization of his lust causing her own to ignite.

Her head swam. Instinctively, her fingers wrapped around his hardness and began an avid exploration of the smooth length. Her heart leapt when Gareth's face tightened, his eyelids drooping with unmistakable pleasure. His fingers still covered hers, not urging movement but following her hand as it slipped down to the root and then traveled upward, learning every ridge along the way before rising to capture the bulbous head in her fist.

He moaned and his hips jerked, his cock pulsing hard, once, within the tight grip of her hand. Mary clenched her thighs together, the flesh between them echoing the thrum of need she'd felt through her fingers.

Gareth wants me.

And seemingly with a need that matched her own.

His expression of arousal was so stark, so overwhelming, it eclipsed everything, leaving nothing in the world but him.

"Let me go, Mary. *Please.*"

Instead, she tightened her grip, loath to release him. Yet doubt snaked through her too.

Plain, she'd been called repeatedly. *Thin*, even *wizened*. It wasn't only her first husband who'd opined she wasn't plump enough to be of interest to any man. How could Gareth want her?

Her fingers loosened, but now Gareth held them in place. "What?"

The fierce edge to his tone startled her, causing a wave of cold to wash over her skin. She shook her head, unwilling to give voice to either her desire or her fear.

"Do you not believe me?"

Something in his eyes told her he would not be denied. And her heart told her that if there was to be any hope of happiness between them she must be honest, although it stung her pride to give voice to her thoughts. She lifted her chin, blinking against the tears pricking her eyes. "I know I am not comely, my lord. Indeed, all my life I have been called plain. How can I believe you desire me?"

The flare of anger in his eyes made her heart leap.

Low voiced, he said, "I have learned 'plain' in one man's eyes can be heavenly in another's. That a warm smile can be more enticing than the most blatant invitation, and a willowy figure can arouse in me the incessant need to touch, to taste, to *take* in a way no buxom wench ever has. If not for my vow never to lie with a woman again, I would keep you in my bed all night, every night, and gorge myself on your sweetness until you begged me leave you be."

Truth rang in his tone, and beneath her fingers his cock was still rigid. In his darkened gaze was all the desire she had ever dreamed of seeing, and more. Awash with need, Mary moved her hand along his length again and said the first words that rose to her lips. "But I am not lying with you."

His eyes widened as his phallus gave another hard pulse against her palm.

Emboldened, she continued. "Indeed, you are sitting. I am kneeling. Your vow remains intact."

Gareth could scarce believe her words and held her wrist to stop her scrambling his thoughts further with the enticing movement of her hand on his cock. Such interpretation of oaths and vows was the purview of clerics. He should take her hand away, he knew, but the pleasure and desire gleaming in her eyes, the sweet way she squeezed and stroked his flesh, was irresistible.

And, suddenly, her interpretation of his vow opened them up to possibilities he doubted Mary had even considered.

Pulling her hand away from his phallus but keeping a grip on her wrist, he heaved to his feet and stepped from the tub.

Rocked back by his sudden movement, Mary stared up at him. Not giving her a chance to speak, he pulled her into his arms. "Now, we are standing," he said, aware of the need deepening his voice to a growl.

And he kissed her, holding nothing back, pouring all the love and longing he'd stored away into her mouth. With her supple body pressed against his and her soft lips opening to welcome the invasion of his tongue, Gareth found a new, glorious torment.

Mary's hands slid all over his skin, each touch making him shudder with heightened arousal. Her heat and scent, the way she mewled so sweetly, took him to the edge of control. Gareth knew there was a line he dared not cross, for if he weren't careful there would come a moment when he would no longer care about the state of his soul.

He carried her to a nearby chair. Breaking the kiss, he looked down into her passion-glazed eyes and knew he was near that point of no return already. She was so beautifully flushed, her lips slightly swollen from his kisses, but he wasn't ready to stop. There was so much he wanted to give her.

Reaching down, he pulled her robe up and over her head, then did the same with her soft linen shift. As her body was revealed Gareth groaned with delight, and couldn't resist letting his fingers trail over the warm flesh from shoulders to breasts, causing her hard nipples to pucker tighter. The sound she made, a gasping moan, brought him untold delight.

When he guided her to sit, she went without protest, and his heart leapt to know she trusted him. Kneeling before her, he parted her thighs and moved between them, leaning forward to place a gentle kiss on her lips.

Then he made love to her the only way he could, seeking out places to please her with his hands, licking and sucking her skin with his mouth. She arched toward him as he worshipped her nipples, driving her fingers into his hair to hold him there, her little cries spurring him on. Then he pulled her bottom closer to the edge of the seat, stretching her out so he could continue his loving assault on her stomach. He heard her little sound of surprise when he moved lower, lured to her most intimate flesh by the sweet scent of arousal, but she made no move to stop him when he spread her legs wide. Looking up into her shocked gaze, he used his tongue to part the lips of her cunt and lick up through them.

Mary's mouth opened with obvious shock, but no sound emerged. Her hips rose, and she shuddered, her fingers tightening in his hair. Knowing he was the first to touch her in this way, Gareth was unable to curtail a smile, and he dipped back to cover her with his mouth, licking and sucking until she went rigid and cried out with release.

As she quieted, Gareth rested his forehead on her stomach,

wrestling with his own desire. Oh, how he wanted to be inside her, the need clawing at him like a dragon trying to tear through his chest. He dared not even put a finger into her wet heat for fear the sensation would drive him to forget what little scruples he still possessed.

Mary tugged on his hair, and he raised his head to meet her soft gaze.

"Let me help you, my lord." She sat up, her hand sliding down his chest and belly, until her fingertips touched the head of his cock. "Let me give you back some measure of what you just gave me."

Unable to resist, Gareth rested against her shoulder and let her take him into her hand and caress his aching flesh. As pleasure slipped to the cusp of pain, and then swung wildly back to ecstasy, he knew somehow, even if it cost everything he had, he would one day possess this woman fully, completely.

Mary fell asleep on Gareth's lap, curled up against his chest, sated and stunned by what they'd done, yet still wanting more. Never before had she known such delight. Never had she dreamed she could crave another with such ferocity.

When she awoke alone in her own bed, she wondered if she'd imagined the entire encounter. Yet, she knew she hadn't, and she rushed through her ablutions to see Gareth all the sooner.

Her heart broke on receiving word he was gone, taking only his guardsman with him—the destination and duration of his journey unknown by any at the keep.

She kept her head high, but inside was a mass of pain that refused to abate. Indeed, it grew with each day that passed, until on the sixth day of his absence she didn't want to lift her head from her pillow.

The sound of the door opening only made her murmur, "I will arise soon."

"No," came the reply. "Stay where you are, my lady, for it is my wish to join you."

"Gareth!" Sitting up, seeing him stripping off his clothing, made her heart leap. "You have returned."

"Of course." He paused, surveying her closely. "Did you think I wouldn't?"

"You left no word...I didn't know..."

"I am poor with the quill and knew what needed saying could not be entrusted to another." Still in his hose and tunic, he came to sit on the bed and took her hands in his. "I rode to Sawley Abbey, seeking the Abbot's counsel on whether the oath I spoke could somehow be nullified."

Heart pounding, Mary could only whisper, "What did he say?"

Gareth smiled, his face alight with love and happiness, but Mary couldn't smile in return, too shaken by his sudden appearance and desperate to hear his news.

Squeezing her fingers, Gareth said, "I was young and had lost the woman I wanted to another. I vowed she was the wife of my heart, and I would lie with no other, lest I prove faithless. When I told the Abbot that Lizbeth had died even before I came back from the Holy Land, he said I had upheld my oath long enough, and now, I am as a widower would be, free to be a fitting husband to you. He did stipulate that I make an offering each year to the church to show I appreciated the dispensation I received. I can now make you mine in body, as I already have in my heart, and freely vow to be yours, forever." His eyes darkened as he added, "'Twill be the easiest of vows to keep."

Oh, how sweet his words sounded! How beautiful was the day and the man who had given her back her joy and hope for the future. Mary lay down on the pillows, pulling his unresisting body with her. Against his questing lips, she murmured, "'Tis an oath I make with you, my love, and promise never to break."

Poetry and Amber

Axa Lee

Along the Volga River, 899 AD

I woke naked under furs, the smell of wood smoke and water from the river in my nose, one leg slung over the waist of a Northman. Our hair mixed on the pillow, his bleached bone, mine like fire, our skins equally pale. He slumbered on, the great, long, scarred body all smooth, warm muscle against me. I loved the long length of his back. Since the first moment I laid eyes on him, I could become entranced watching him bend and flex or sluice himself with salt water for a bath. It's the feature that won me to him. A long back, strong arms, and shocking eyes—raptor sharp and the color of a changing sky. That was ten years ago.

Shouts outside rose in alarm then subsided.

Tartars were still frightened of us in this part of the world. While they might attack and slaughter caravans, they remained cautious about attacking Rus ships.

I couldn't help myself and curled in closer along the line

of his back, so that my body traveled the length of his. His heat suffused me and I wanted him again, that cock filling me, wanted to put more nail marks along the lovely pale plane.

Outside our tent, the camp stirred. Thralls and younger women with small children stirred the fires and carried water from the river. We were a loose camp of maybe a dozen ships, returning west from our new settlement, summoned back by the king of kings. We'd been ten years in the east, carving out an outpost for trade in amber and furs, creating peace so trade might flourish, extending even as far south as Constantinople.

"How do you create peace?" I'd asked him.

Buliwyf had laid his hand on his sword in answer.

The warrior beside me stirred. Still half-asleep, he rolled to his back and hauled me against him. He said he liked how I felt against him, the size of me. One of his wives had been so small he'd worried about hurting her. But he and I were of a size, my eyes level with his nose, and we were, I imagined, a striking couple.

"What do you see?" Buliwyf asked, voice thick from sleep.

"Your cock in my mouth," I might have said, as I often did. Or, "You fucking me, with my cunt so wet it's as though I'm crying." Instead, what I said was, "Trouble."

Ten Years Earlier

At the funeral of the old king, amidst the smells of roasted lambs, beer and honey mead, I was presented before the heirs apparent with a curt shove in their general direction. I met the gazes of the Northmen fearlessly, letting them chatter as they would about my various attributes, all but displaying my teeth like a mare. They even turned me around, so the heirs' eyes might rest on my tattoos. To them, my tattoos meant bravery, whereas to me, as my mother told me, they signaled wisdom.

One of the heirs' gazes caught on the pendant at my throat. It was a raw crystal, strung on a leather thong with onyx beads. I let him look as he wished, and I looked back. Then I wished I hadn't.

I'd been too long in the south and had lost my taste for dark-haired men. This man was fair, not one of the dark, ruddy Northmen. Buliwyf was a big man, imposing in a fight, I imagined, with his broad shoulders and wicked long reach. If he was quick enough. By the devouring nature of his gaze, noticing everything, I imagined him very quick.

His gaze made me shiver. Want for him rose so swiftly, so unexpectedly, that my knees almost buckled. I didn't like him, didn't know him, but I wanted him. I wanted this warrior spread naked beneath me, to feel those hard muscles tense as he seized hold of me, to buck against me as I rode him by firelight.

Still staring at my throat, he pointed and said a word I did not know.

"*Volva*," he said again. The word was guttural and harsh, unlike the language of the Celts and Picts. More like the low tongue spoken by the Saxons. In my opinion.

"Magic," he said. "Do you have visions? Like the ones on your back?"

He appeared to be quite drunk, wavering where he sat, his long blond hair spilling loose about his shoulders. The easy physicality of this man entranced me. I'd never been so drawn to a man at first sight, never wanted him so completely within such a short time. He was a warrior embodied, a god of war made flesh.

A slave girl, a thrall, bent to refill his cup. She leaned a little too close, angling her body across his, touching him longer than she needed to. Just then, the other heir apparent made his move. The thrall exclaimed as she was shoved aside. His sword flashed.

Buliwyf moved faster. He was not, apparently, as drunk as he had appeared. He was on his feet, sword drawn, blocking that of his opponent. As I'd expected, Buliwyf fought well. He fought like a dream, like one born with his hand around a sword. I could not tell where the sword ended and the swordsman began.

As suddenly as the fight began, it stilled. For a moment, the combatants stared at each other. Buliwyf's sword flashed, and the other man fell.

Then, and only then, after the heads fell and the meal was blessed by the shedding of blood, Buliwyf straightened, barely winded from slaying the other contender to the crown. His eyes locked with mine, and he raised two fingers, beckoning me to him.

My cunt pulsed for him.

"You are *volva*?"

He used that word again. I still didn't know what it meant. I shook my head. "I don't know that word."

Buliwyf drank deeply from the cup of his fallen opponent. Then he plucked a golden armband from his forearm and tossed it to one of the men standing nearby. He said something in a rough voice that roughly translated to "I have paid for him."

I remembered someone saying once that if a Northman kills another Northman, the death-price must be paid. It was the mark of a good king. By the nods of approval from around the tent at the action of the new king, this must have been the case. Slowly, the music and drone of voices resumed, and the body was removed from the tent.

"Come," Buliwyf said, gesturing to the place beside him.

I sat and drank deep from an offered cup of sweet honey mead. The alcohol made my head spin.

"They tell me you have magic, that you make things happen," he said. "Is this true?"

Was that why he'd accepted their gift of me? I wondered. Or would admitting magic sentence me to the same fate as the old king? Rus were superstitious, I'd heard.

"Mind your tongue," the old one had warned me, as we walked from our camp to that of the Northmen. "With luck, you'll fuck a king tonight. Without luck, well, you'll still be *with* a king. But you'll be following him into hell." Northmen burned the bodies of their dead kings. I had no desire to "travel" with him to the underworld. She'd cackled then, like the old crone she was, and I'd gritted my teeth to resist cursing her with more boils than she already had.

Rather than answer, I leaned across Buliwyf to let the thrall, the one who'd been shoved out of the way of the fight, refill my cup. She did, grudgingly, and seemed to pout that she couldn't drape herself across the new king's shoulders.

As I leaned back, Buliwyf caught my left hand in his.

I bit my lip. I'd done well to hide this particular defect during the initial display. Now he'd see my deformity and consign me to the ship with the old king.

He took my maimed left hand in both of his. My hands were already small, but with the left one having only the smallest finger whole and the rest sliced off at an angle, only a nubbin of thumb remaining, his hands appeared giant in comparison.

He cradled my maimed hand, turning it this way and that, studying it. "A grievous injury," he said very seriously. "What happened?"

He seemed genuinely interested, looking me in the eyes, attention fixed on me. You could get lost in his eyes. He'd just killed a man, but cradled my hand like a thin-shelled egg.

"It...I..." I licked my lips and drank my mead instead.

With the music, revelry had returned to the tent. Women's shrill laughter cut through the smoky air, joined by the raucous laughter and loud jokes of men. The tent was ripe with the smell of bodies and crisp meat. These were a virile people, who believed in fire and laughter and drinking. The men had big laughs, broad shoulders, big horses and big weapons.

I hoped at least the one beside me had a big cock to match. The thought, welling up unbidden, much like my desire for him, made my cheeks heat. From Buliwyf's amused half smile as he watched me, I blushed.

It was a camp teeming with fighting-fit, cold-forged warrior-traders who sought their fortune in the east, with tattoos across some of their faces, men with long hair, thick beards, deep chuckles, loud jokes, sharp swords and hard saddles. They told stories, laughed and fucked like it was the last days of their lives. For, like their gods, I think they believed that every day might be.

"Our..." he said a word in Rus I didn't know. "Angel of death," he explained, "you would call her an oracle, flew to the gods this winter past. My reign won't be secure until I have another."

My cunt throbbed. I could barely concentrate on what Buliwyf was saying. It didn't matter what he said. I just wanted those lips to be moving, preferably on my belly, then my hips, then lower...

"What makes you think I have this power?" I asked.

He gestured to my hand. "What other good are you? With

half a hand. You are a witch or you are a whore." He didn't mean to be insulting, merely spoke the truth. He nodded toward the men who had given me to him, an offering so he wouldn't burn their village or rape their women. "They are wise and know that *I*...need both."

Past the distracting pulsing and spreading dampness between my legs, I realized I hadn't expected this man to be intelligent. A keen fighter, yes, but as we conversed, I realized he was a man actually worth talking to. Not just a man, a king.

He still held my maimed hand. When I attempted to remove it from his grasp, his hold tightened. He kissed the ends of my missing fingers, his mouth light. He turned my wrist over and delicately ran his tongue over the pulse point there, keeping his eyes locked with mine.

My hand spasmed, and he smiled when my mouth parted and sighed.

Someone called his name, *"BULL-vii,"* and he turned his attention to them, both of them speaking the language of the Rus so quickly I was unable to keep up. The closeness of the air, thick with meat smells and bodies, spilled mead and dirt, affected me suddenly. I rose to my feet and stumbled from the tent. I'd never been so wet.

The air outside was crisp and cool. A mist settled in over the river. I heard some nervous mutterings from the few gathered around the fire outside as they eyed the mist. They didn't like it, that much was sure. But whether for reasons of travel or super-stition, I didn't know.

I'd never been so affected by anyone as I was by this Rus king. And so quickly. The fierceness of the desire had startled me, shaken me to my core. Every part of such instantaneous lust felt wrong, but for some inexplicable reason, I trusted it. I

trusted him. The tone of his voice and how he looked at me...
Somehow, I felt sure of him.

The atmosphere back inside the tent had, if anything, grown wilder. Several men copulated with willing slave girls, though many warriors sagged along the low tables, heavily drunk. The noise level had risen, reaching a crescendo of drunken revelry. The musicians played more and more wrong chords, and the listeners noticed less and less, as they shouted to be heard above one another's drink-induced deafness.

Buliwyf's conversation had ended, and he remained seated at the low table. The thrall who'd served us all evening had at last succeeded in draping herself across his lap.

My face burned. As I watched, she kissed him, fumbling at the front of his pants with the hand not tangled in his hair.

My face flushed. It was too much. To be traded to barbarians was bad enough, but to be supplanted by a mere thrall, that was truly intolerable. I wanted him. I was wet for him. I was not about to let the little thrall retire with my new master, leaving me to spend my first night writhing against my own hand, whispering his name, my lip clenched between my teeth.

I took matters upon myself.

I strode over to them and took the girl by the arm, pulling her to her feet. Her mouth was red and swollen, her eyes wide and confused. I did the only thing I could think of under the circumstances.

I kissed her.

It was a long kiss, and first, I tasted her shock. As I rolled my tongue against hers, she responded.

Despite the festive nature of the tent, we drew notice. I pulled back from the girl, smiling mischievously at her amidst the noise. I reached down a hand to Buliwyf, who rose to his feet, draped an arm across either of our shoulders, and, to the boisterous calls and ribald suggestions of his men, propelled us out of the tent.

Buliwyf's tent had a small fire and a camp bed of sleeping furs and wool blankets. His eyes darkened with desire, and his mouth twitched with a curious smile. He reclined on the bed, granting me permission to continue as I would.

My hands shook as I unclipped the girl's brooches so her outer dress slipped to the ground. Her headscarf was already askew. I tugged it off, and she shook out a head of thick blond hair.

"I am Cajsa," she said.

I didn't care. I ran my fingertips down the side of her face, over the swell of one breast. She breathed rapidly, making little puffs of fog inside the tent. My own breathing was quick as well. I'd never done this before, never touched another woman this way, but as I glanced at Buliwyf, watching, there was no way I'd back down now.

I let my fingers trace her collarbone then down the curve of her breast. I bent and took one of her pink nipples into my mouth. The flesh responded, hardening beneath my tongue. It felt strange, and then it didn't, as I licked and suckled gently. She dropped her head back and sighed. I moved to the other breast, fingers brushing over her bare body. She shivered and clenched my shoulders, nails marking my skin.

Kneeling, I kissed lower, lips and tongue moving across her hips and the sensitive skin between her thighs. She was wet, I found, and she groaned, clenching my shoulders harder when I stroked her cunt. She clenched my hand between her thighs, biting her lip.

I heard Buliwyf rise, felt his lips on the vulnerable nape of my neck. He brushed his mouth down the bare slope of my shoulder, and I shivered. He bit down.

Cajsa and I arched, both exclaiming in pleasure.

He kissed down my shoulder, sliding my dress off until it puddled around my ankles.

I knelt between Cajsa and our king in nothing but my crystal pendant.

Buliwyf began stroking me, mirroring how I touched Cajsa, so both of us writhed and panted, feeling what the other felt. A building began within me, a great pressure. I bucked against his hand, as Cajsa bucked against mine, wet, so wet, sopping, wet as I'd ever been, and we were almost there, almost satisfied, almost...

Buliwyf removed his hand. I exclaimed in mixed surprise and frustration.

He drew me to my feet and sat me on the bed with a look that said, *Stay there.*

He tugged Cajsa to the bed also, and she reacted the way that I wanted to, willingly falling to her hands and knees, ass in the air.

I watched, mouth suddenly dry, cunt aching, as Buliwyf ran his hand over Cajsa's ass, then slapped it, hard enough to make her jump, to leave a red mark on her pale skin. He grunted, a sound that made me quiver, and took hold of either side of Cajsa's hips, pulling her into him, ramming her hips with his. His cock was as large as I'd hoped for and eager as it pressed against Cajsa's earnest backside. She wriggled, arched against him, asking for more.

I wanted to weep, as he dragged his cock across her willing slit. Was this my punishment for being damaged? Forced to watch as the man I wanted took another woman? Was I that repelling with my witch-red hair and half hand?

Don't touch yourself, his body language seemed to say, *don't you dare touch yourself.*

It physically hurt to watch them together. I wanted so much to be in Cajsa's place, to be someone Buliwyf needed, nay, wanted. I wanted him, and worse, I wanted *him* to want *me.*

Just when I was ready to grab my dress and rush from the tent, I noticed Buliwyf. While he still teased Cajsa, he'd not begun fucking her. He teased her cunt, with fingers and the end of his cock, until the girl shook, rocking and sighing, her movements growing frenzied, until she stiffened, shuddered once, twice, biting back her cries, then slowly sank onto the wool and furs.

I didn't want to watch this. I wanted it to be me his cock was buried in, me he brought to violent ecstasy, not her.

Cajsa's heavy breathing slowed. She rolled to her back, looking up first at Buliwyf then at me.

He was still watching me. He'd been watching me the whole time, watching my frustration, my jealousy, my desire. He wanted me to feel that. He was trying to show me something, promise me something. He was, I realized, doing this for me.

"I need an Angel of Death," he'd said.

He wanted me, I realized, and he wanted me to want him. And more, he wanted me to know how badly I wanted him. Not just as his concubine, but as his witch.

Buliwyf smiled. He'd watched the whole exchange play across my face. I have a glass face.

With a brisk word in the Rus language, he slapped Cajsa on the ass to urge her up. She left, but not without cursing me in murmured yet colorful language.

I raised my eyebrows after she was gone.

Buliwyf chuckled. He waved a hand in dismissal, crossing the room naked, cock still half-aroused and bouncing as he walked. He fetched back two cups of mead.

"She is a thrall," he said. "Cajsa does what she's told."

I took the mead he offered me.

"And what did you tell her?" I eyed him over the edge of my cup.

Buliwyf studied me for a moment then barked a laugh before flopping beside me on the blankets.

"To do whatever you asked of her," he said with a playful smile.

I slapped at him, smiling. Not hard enough to hurt him, but enough to convey my embarrassment.

He laughed and reclined beside me, resting on one elbow. "You see now?" he said.

That mischievous grin had returned. He traced my nipple with one finger, holding his mead in the same hand. I swatted him away, though my breast tingled from his touch. He laughed again and drank.

"I need an oracle," he said.

I ran a finger around the edge of my cup, eyes lowered. "What makes you think me one?" I kept my eyes on him as I drank.

He just looked at me, eyes knowing. He knew what I was, probably better than I did.

"Even if I have...*knowledge*," I stressed this word, "maybe I don't have the power you are looking for."

He tipped my chin up so I had to look at him. He studied my face, my eyes. "What do you see?" he asked. It was a low voice, meant to crawl inside of a woman, to stroke her from the inside out, and it made me shiver.

He was beautiful, even with blood in his hair and battle scars. I ached for him. In that moment, there was nothing I would have denied him. "Wealth," I said at last. "Blood. You go east to raid, yes?"

"I go east to trade. There is great wealth in furs and amber. My land will go to my sons, and my wealth and glory lies down the river." He clenched his jaw, lips pressed hard together.

I laid my hand on his arm. I didn't see every time I touched someone else. There had to be a certain level of empathy, of trust.

The vision came in bursts. Windswept lands, stunted trees. Hairy cattle and horned sheep grazing short-season grass. A boy. He ran around the cottage, swinging a too-long sword. But the scene receded, as though the person through whose eyes I saw were traveling away from it.

I blinked several times. The scene faded, and I returned to a smoky tent, looking into the eyes of a king.

"What did you see?"

I had the strangest feeling he already knew. I told him.

Buliwyf sighed and lay back against the furs, resting his head on one arm, holding his cup with the other, staring at the ceiling.

"I have a wife. I won't return to them." He sounded grim. "There is nothing for me there." He took a deep breath. "But you are here. And I am here. You are strong, I think. I want our lives to be here. Together." He paused. "You know you make me very happy."

I melted.

"As you do me." I bit his shoulder. I didn't want to ask it, but I did anyway. "Is he your son?"

He was slow to answer. I didn't really need him to answer. I rose and threw a leg over him, straddling his half-erect cock.

His eyes widened at feeling how wet I still was.

"I see things," I admitted. "Sometimes. I can cast bones and read futures in palms. I can cure skin afflictions and draw down fevers. I know the plants to use to rouse a man's desires and herbs women take to cast out an unwanted child. They called me witch. They sold me to you because they believe I'm cursed and draw devils down on them."

"Did you?"

I snorted. "Not on purpose."

He smiled.

And then the smile faded. Our eyes lingered. He drew me down to him, and he kissed me.

His mouth was gentler than I would have expected. He didn't maul me, but skimmed his lips across mine, flicking my tongue with his and withdrawing. It was sensual, unhurried, such a contrast to how he had been with Cajsa.

In that moment, the past and future blurred. I was kissing him for the first time, yet it felt like the thousandth. I knew just what he wanted, and he anticipated me, hands slipping over my body, mouth hot on mine. We writhed and gasped against each other, and when he backed me into him, when he slapped my ass, when he finally entered me, the world stopped.

"*Inn matki munr,*" he whispered against the back of my neck. He entwined his fingers with mine as he thrust into me, while I lay prone on my belly. He bit the back of my neck, and both of us went still.

Roughly translated, it meant "the mighty passion." We felt it even then, as we paused in our lovemaking for him to press me to him, as though he would draw me into himself, protect me from harm and cherish my body. It was easier for men, I thought, especially Northmen, to speak of such things, of love, of passion, of what we might build. Men are supposed to espouse poetry like their one-eyed god. And men had the option of who to love and when. But in this case, with this man, with this *king*, maybe I had a choice too. Somehow, I felt, the choice had already been made.

He began to fuck me slowly, so the tremors built and when they crested, in surge after body-wracking surge, when I lay beneath him after, languid like melted candle wax, he whispered something. I didn't understand it at first. Then, I thought he might be singing. It was an ugly growling sound, like all Rus music, but the words were beautiful.

"Happy am I to have won the joy of such a consort; I shall not go down basely in loneliness to the gods of Tartarus."

"What do you see?" he asked.

I blinked. "I see gold. And burning cities."

He chuckled. "You are a smart slut to tell me so." He rolled onto his side, grabbed a handful of my ass and squeezed. Then his hand slipped lower, his fingers dipped into me.

My lips parted as I gasped, clutching his shoulders involuntarily.

"What do you really see?"

I closed my eyes. I saw fighting and fire, blood on gold, fresh thralls and fat sows being herded aboard our ships.

Buliwyf removed his hand and replaced it with his cock. My breath caught as I struggled not to lose my concentration.

I saw white water and steaming mountains.

"Please," I whispered.

I saw a warrior and riches.

"'Please'?" He moved again, hitting that spot so I came again.

Almost against my will, I shuddered beneath him. I saw ships and gold and dragons.

"Please," I begged, "I want you to come inside me."

His breath was hot next to my ear.

"What do you see?" he said.

"I see babies," I whispered, and his mouth slanted hot across mine as he spilled his seed inside me, the pleasure from his coming bringing me along all over again. And then, I saw poetry.

THE SQUIRE

Cela Winter

Northern France, 1346 AD

...$\mathcal{E}$*t Spiritus Sancti. Amen.*"

Godfrey crossed himself, one of a handful of mourners standing beside the mass burial pit. Poor Hugo. His faithful squire, felled by a foe worse than the hated French—camp fever. The flux killed more soldiers than arrow or sword.

No use dawdling. Many chores, normally tended by the squire, awaited. He turned from the grave and found his way blocked by a young man who bowed and bent the knee.

"God give you good day. Are you Sir Godfrey of Chriswell?"

"I am. Who seeks to know?"

The speaker arose. Godfrey eyed the beardless chin and narrow shoulders beneath the leather jerkin; not a man, but a lad, no more than a stripling.

"Wulfric, squire to Sir Ranulf of Fairfield."

"I know him not. What is his business with me?"

"We are newly come to France, sir." He took a shaking

breath. "Now he lies in yon hole, dead. But my purpose in disturbing your own grief, sir, is—" The words stumbled out. "I was hoping, well, you have lost your squire and I my master—" The youth's voice broke, and his face reddened, but he held Godfrey's gaze steadfast.

The knight looked down into the blue-green eyes. The boy was so young, bereft of his master, alone in a hostile country. And there was something more there, a tantalizing sense of recognition he could not define...

Godfrey dismissed the notion and made a hasty decision. "I've a meeting with Earl Richard, who is my liege—and now yours. Bring your things to my tent. The pennant is red and white quartered with a yellow rising sun."

"I will serve you well, sir, I vow," the boy called after Godfrey, then watched his new master striding away through the camp.

All around them were the sounds of an army on the move— the creak of leather harnesses, whip cracks, curses and shouts, the muffled clop of hooves. Wulfric coughed in the dust and sighed.

"Aye, lad. This too is a soldier's life, yet you'll hear neither ballad nor drinking song about a weary march," Godfrey remarked, watching the boy pull his neckerchief up over his mouth and nose.

The knight shifted in the saddle, trying to rid his sense of unease. Not fear of the battle to which they marched, soon or late, but the disturbing consciousness of his squire. He had no real fault to find; several weeks together had shown the boy to be well-bred and well trained, with a ready wit and deft in his service—indeed, he added much to Godfrey's comfort that Hugo never had. But there was something rather…queer about him.

He went missing at odd times, though never for long and always with an excuse. Whenever Godfrey tried to draw him out about his family or past, he would shift the conversation. After that unsettling look at their first meeting, the boy kept his gaze down—a most unmanly habit. Yet, perversely, the knight had an instinctive liking and trust for the lad.

What he did not trust were his own feelings toward the squire. He found himself studying the lad, noticing his walk and bearing. One day at weapon practice, he'd gripped the boy's shoulder and been startled at the delicacy of the bones beneath the mail shirt. His hand had burned for hours thereafter.

For the first time, Godfrey came to dread evening, when it was just the two of them in the tent. At times, he could scarce lie still on his camp bed, the nearness of his companion drawing him like a lodestone. Sleep was a torment of fragmented dreams involving flesh, firm muscles and that red-lipped mouth. Many nights he fled their shared tent, seeking relief at his own hand— something he would have to admit to his confessor, again.

A lifelong soldier, he was well aware of unseemly intimacies between certain men. Women were often scarce, apart from the doxies who followed the camps. Any man who valued his parts, not to mention his purse, would do well to stay away. Godfrey was as lusty as any man, but if a clean—and willing—woman were not available, he did without. As a man of honor, he would not stoop to ravish the womenfolk of those they conquered.

Wulfric made him doubt all that he knew of himself.

Mayhap it was time to quit soldiering. He'd been well rewarded for his service over the years with estates he seldom visited. He tried to imagine manor life, with farms and tenants, always in the same place. Could he adapt to that existence?

He would marry, of course, a lass of good family with lands to increase his, someone to grace his table, warm his bed and produce heirs. It was the sensible thing to do.

Somehow, the mental picture of the unknown bride-to-be had Wulfric's sea-colored eyes and red hair.

Christ's Wounds! Would death in battle be the only way to cleanse his mind of such thoughts, to rid his body of its appetite? The lad was driving him mad.

"Boy!"

Wulfric looked up, startled by his curt tone.

"Ride ahead and see about tonight's camp. 'Tis likely the Earl will call a meeting at the halt. I expect all to be ready when we're done."

The squire nodded in deference and kicked his horse to a faster pace. Godfrey observed again that the boy sat his horse well; his thighs were lean but well muscled, rounding sleekly into the arse... He stopped that line of thought abruptly.

Yes, marriage—and soon.

The boy lost no time obeying orders. Belongings stowed and the horses picketed, the squire strolled casually into a wooded area as if to stretch his legs.

He glanced around, before fumbling beneath his tunic and extracting a peculiar object from a pouch tied around the waist. It was a glazed clay funnel, pinkish and shaped like a man's penis. After fitting it betwixt her legs, Lady Wilfreda of Fairfield sighed as the stream hit the ground. Praise Heaven there were some days before she need deal with the additional difficulties of monthly rags.

Shaking out the last drops, she carefully stowed the funnel away; it was vital to her deception. The thought of what could happen if she were found out, an unattended woman in a military camp, was not something to dwell upon. She'd never thought to find herself alone, without Ranulf's protection. Lacking his help, she wasn't sure how long she could continue without discovery.

Her heart ached for him, hating his ignominious death. Reality was a far cry from the adventure the two of them had planned; neither anticipated that he would die without ever swinging a sword.

Enough. The time for grieving would be later.

Wilfreda squared her shoulders and left the wood, a boy once more.

The battle would be at dawn in two days' time. The French had the advantage of numbers, the English the benefit of terrain and a day to rest whilst the enemy still marched. Godfrey strode through the encampment, his head full of the upcoming engagement, stopping short some paces from his destination.

Wulfric sat outside their tent in a meager slice of shade; the heat had finally forced him to remove the ungainly leather jerkin. He bent over a mail hauberk spread across his legs, buffing away spots of rust. The collar of the undertunic he wore slipped to one side, revealing a space where tanned skin met white. The boy's neck was a slender as a girl's. The knight's tongue twitched with desire to trace that bi-colored line of flesh then follow the little knobs of the spine down and down... God's Blood!

"Set that aside. Bring the practice swords to yon clearing. Let us ready ourselves for the French."

Mayhap some hard exercise would help.

* * *

The day's ride followed by a punishing round of sword practice should have tired her out, but Wilfreda found herself sleepless, alight inside with her awareness of Godfrey lying a hand's span away.

It wasn't just his handsome face or battle prowess that caused her yearning; he was everything a knight should be—noble, pious, kind. It nigh broke her heart to rebuff his attempts to befriend the squire he believed her to be.

A woman's lust was greater than a man's, 'twas common knowledge, but her craving for Godfrey shocked her. It was nothing like her feeling for Ranulf—making love with him had been but a delicious game. This was entirely different.

Living so closely with a man, with *Godfrey*, was awkward in more ways than just the ruse she maintained. That evening, he'd casually whipped off his linen shirt and used it to wipe the sweat from the back of his neck. It was such an ordinary gesture, one any man might make. Why did it affect her so? When he turned away, she lifted the shirt to her face, breathing in the man-scent of him.

Seeing him walk about their shared tent half-naked set her to imagining how his hard muscles would feel under her hands, his weight on top of her... She struggled with the longing to reveal her secret, in part to share the burden of it, but mainly for him to know her as a woman.

What if she rolled over and pressed her body to his? What if she took his hand, placed it on her breast, and—

Godfrey gave a low groan as he rose from his bed and stumbled outside.

With a moment of unexpected privacy, her hand stole to her quim. As she caressed herself, her mind drifted in dreamy exploration of Godfrey's body and his reaction. How the firm column of his throat would feel beneath her lips, his hiss as she tongued his red-brown nipples, the way he would groan when she slipped her hand down his *brais* to cup his balls and stroke his cock to readiness.

Her fingers sped up as, in the fantasy, he pressed her down onto her pallet, covering her mouth, neck and breasts with hard kisses, before thrusting a knee between her thighs and lowering himself on top of her. She slid two fingers inside herself, then a third, wishing with all her heart for Godfrey's girth filling her and his powerful strength pounding at her womb. Gritting her teeth, she rode out her climax in silence.

When he reentered the tent, she forced her breathing to slow. With a heavy sigh—what could trouble him so?—he lay down. Slowly, she drifted to sleep, hand still between her legs, aware of him even in her dreams.

Rhythmic huffs and grunts, cries and exclamations. The smell of blood and dust and shite.

Why was he lying on the ground? Godfrey's head swam sickeningly as he tried to rise then fell back. He squinted against the bright sky above, aware of movement in his peripheral vision.

"For Godfrey of Chriswell!" It was Wulfric, his voice shrill with effort, sounding a battle cry as he wielded his sword two-handed, protecting his fallen master.

There was something about that voice he should recognize, Godfrey thought as he drifted into darkness once more...

"A-a bath? Is that really necessary?"

Godfrey regarded his squire with exasperation. "Why so obstinate? Tomorrow you are to be dubbed a knight. You cannot go before Earl Richard, or the Almighty, unless you are clean in body and spirit. Confession—followed by hot water and soap." Refreshed by his own earlier bath, he spoke with certitude.

"Er, yes, sir. But I can manage on my own, truly."

"It is my privilege to attend you this night as you have so often served me, Wulfric. I could do no less for the man who saved my life." Fine words as he silently cursed the tradition. How much of the throbbing in his head was due to the blow he'd taken in battle, and how much to the prospect of seeing his squire naked?

"Let us hear no more about it. Strip." Godfrey ducked under the tent flaps to where a kettle of water steamed over the open fire. "Consider it another test of your knighthood." He tossed the words over his shoulder.

The habit of obedience had Wilfreda's hand tugging at the ties of the jerkin even as her mind formulated more excuses and protests. Should she crawl under the back wall of the tent and run? Then what? Risk discovery? Try to find another knight somewhere, one who wasn't Sir Godfrey? At the thought, pain squeezed her heart like a fist.

Come what may, Godfrey would hardly offer her violence or assault. It was time to end the charade. The decision made, she felt light-headed with relief as she yanked the jerkin then the undertunic over her head and tossed them aside. The *brais* and woolen hose were next. Fumbling in her haste, she unwound the linen bandage that flattened her breasts.

Completely bare for the first time in months, her skin was acutely sensitive, and she shivered in the warm air. The discomfort of being so covered up in the summer heat had nearly defeated her disguise many a time. And to *wash*, to be free of grime and sweat at last... It would be worth whatever reaction Godfrey might have. She stepped into the shallow bathing pan, eager to come clean, in more ways than one.

Godfrey was speaking as he came back in, shouldering aside the loose canvas. "'Tis a pity that you can't be dubbed a little closer to home, where your family might—"

He stopped short, a wave of hot water from the kettle sloshing over his naked feet. His eyes darted over her body, clearly not believing what he beheld.

Wilfreda would have found the parade of emotions on his face humorous, if not for the disquiet twisting her insides. Puzzlement, a touch of anger, and...relief. *Why?* she wondered.

"By the Holy Mother's Tears! You're a-a-a woman!"

He circled her, still examining, and she felt the old humiliation of being too tall and too strong, not a *proper* girl as her family told her time and again. She began to droop in the thick silence.

"How could I be so blind?" he breathed.

The tension shifted, leaving her giddy—and daring. "Weren't you going to help me wash, Sir Godfrey?" She straightened, holding out the wooden dish of soft soap as a prompt.

"Oh. Ah, yes." He stepped behind her.

She held still as water splashed. She heard a swish, then the wringing of a cloth.

The trickle of water from the dipper down her back puckered her nipples. Godfrey went to work on her shoulders with the soapy rag, tentatively at first, then harder as she leaned into the pressure of his hand.

"So what do I call you?" he asked quietly. "You surely weren't christened Wulfric."

"Wilfreda."

"Pretty. How did you come to be here, Wilfreda? Was there really a Sir Ranulf?"

"Ye-es." She tried to pull her thoughts together to make the tale coherent; the knight's touch was distracting her. "He was honored by our liege for his prowess in several tournaments."

Godfrey gave a snort, showing what he thought of titles bestowed to men untested by battle. "And this tourney knight, Ranulf, thought it a fine idea to bring a *maiden* as his squire? Or not a maid, I suppose, but a—"

"Not a maiden, no," she interrupted, "and no doxie either. I was his wife, now his widow."

"That makes even less sense. What kind of man brings his wife to war?"

"One whose wife won't stay home. It was...my idea."

"I should be surprised, but somehow I'm not." He rinsed her back with the dipper, the suds making rivulets down her legs to the bath pan.

"Hold out your arm." He started with her hand, working up over her elbow to her underarm. His fingers, holding the cloth, brushed the side of her breast.

Wilfreda felt a lightning stroke from that point of contact. She gave a sidelong glance over her shoulder. Godfrey's face was determined and absorbed, but there was a faint sheen of sweat across his brow. Not caused, she thought, merely by the weather.

"Pray, go on with this fantastic tale." His tone was gruff.

"I knew Ranulf always, you see, our family holdings adjoin. We grew up together, and he was ever my favorite playmate. Instead of sewing and spinning, I would borrow my brother's clothes and run off with him to play at boys' games. Thus I learned to fight and shoot, practicing under his family's master-at-arms."

Arms finished, Godfrey squatted down, which brought him level with her buttocks. He paused for a moment before starting on her legs. His ministrations took on a different feel, his motions now slower, each pass with the cloth longer, more searching. He placed a hand on her hip as if to steady her.

Wilfreda wondered if her growing arousal was evident. "My mother would weep, saying no man could want such a hoyden for a bride. Father threatened beatings, but it never stopped me. They were both so relieved when Ranulf offered for my hand, Father couldn't say yes fast enough. And so we wed.

"Ranulf wanted more than anything to truly serve His Majesty and help to reclaim the lands stolen by the French. And I-I wanted an adventure, a memory to hold when I put aside my boyish ways and became a proper wife."

Godfrey huffed under his breath.

"So I cut off my hair and persuaded him to bring me as his squire. We took ship and—" Her head bent under the weight of grief and shame. "I talked him into it—and now he's dead."

The knight stood and moved around to face her. "Wilfreda, look at me." When she could not, he lifted her chin with a finger. His expression was both solemn and sympathetic, with something else there that made her heart speed up. "We all feel guilt, we who survive. Don't blame yourself so harshly. Ranulf knew the risks of war; he still wished to come. He could well have died in any case."

"Yes, but—"

"Hush." He was standing very close to her now. "I think your backside is as clean as it can be."

Overcome, Wilfreda dropped her gaze. There was a noticeable bulge from under the long linen shirt that was all he wore.

He brought the cloth to her neck, water from it dripping over her breasts. "What are these marks on your skin?"

"They're from the swaddling bands I used." The words had to squeeze past a lump of desire in her throat. The cloth moved gently over the red creases, then lower to her belly.

Godfrey's voice sounded strained as he asked, "Did you love him greatly?"

She chose her words with care. "It was a-a childish love between playfellows, one of comradeship and happy memories. Unlike the others in my life, Ranulf never judged me. I will miss that."

Wilfreda stepped from the pan onto the groundsheet to stand a mere finger's breadth from the knight. She looked up into his eyes, feeling a welcome, unfamiliar shock of being *smaller-than*. "Yet, I did not know, till lately, what it was to love...a man."

She raised one hand to cup his jaw; with the other she plucked away the washcloth and guided his palm to curve around her breast. "Godfrey, you will think me the hoyden my mother decried, but I must-must..." Words failed and her face burned, matching the heat in her quim.

"The girl who came to war...wants me." He was so close she could feel his breath on her face. He bent nearer, brushing her lips with his, while his thumb made lazy circles around her nipple.

Rings of sensation rippled through her like a pebble dropped in a still pond. Her tongue slipped out, first tracing the outline of his lips, then sliding between them.

Their mouths explored, soft and liquid, before turning

fierce, teeth clashing in their hunger. His arm clamped around her waist, pulling her to him, thigh to thigh, belly to belly. All the world was only his body, his hands, his kiss.

Desire swelled through her, and Wilfreda pressed a leg between his, leaning her weight against his wooden cock through the fabric of his shirt. His fingers twined in her short-cropped hair, pulling her head back; teeth nipped at her earlobe, sending a streak of fire straight to her nipples.

"I knew not what to think of myself, these long days and still longer nights, filled with visions of...my squire." His breath was hot in her ear. "I've been nearly mad with want and shame and confusion. The world has righted itself, but now—" He loosed her and stepped back a pace, holding her at arm's length. "Now I've half a mind to throw you to my pallet and serve you as your deception warrants."

He lifted the hem of his shirt and tore it off over his head. Naked, his lust was evident. His cock strained toward her, engorged and glistening.

Wilfreda could feel her face change, reflecting her passion, as she challenged, "Then do that. I want it."

Instantly, he was upon her, bearing her down to the camp bed under his weight. He caught both her wrists in one hand, holding them above her head. In play, she fought against him. The strength she'd always gloried in fueled Godfrey's own passion as they strove against each other.

"'Tis a lusty lass you are." As in her fantasies, he parted her legs with his knees, guiding his hardness to her entrance—then he stopped.

She nearly howled with frustration, but managed by great effort to keep her voice low as she urged, *begged*, "Take me. *Please*, Godfrey!" Still he held back, teasing her breasts with lips and teeth as she writhed, bucking her hips up to him.

He plunged into her. Again she stifled a scream, this one of relief and wanton pleasure. Her legs wrapped around his back, and her fingers dug into his arse, goading him to fill her more deeply still. He pulled back, only his cockhead inside her, then rammed in again. In, out, in, out, the full length of his shaft with every stroke. Drowning in sensation, she began to moan in cadence to his movements.

"Quiet!" Godfrey clapped his hand over her mouth. "You'll have the men lining up for a turn. I'll not share you, Wilfreda. You are mine alone."

Holding her hips, he sat back on his heels and pulled her up onto his thighs, still sheathed inside her and steadily pumping. She stared up at him; a lock of dark hair fluttered against his forehead in rhythm with his thrusts, greedy eyes shifted from her face to her swaying breasts, and then down to where they were joined. His hand cupped her mound, his thumb slipped into her cleft, flicking and rolling her little knot.

She was lost; waves of heat and ecstasy pulsed from her center. Dimly, she felt Godfrey silence her cries with his mouth, his body covering hers once more as he shuddered his release deep within her.

Godfrey woke the following morning to soft sounds in the tent. Wilfreda had gathered her—Wulfric's—mail armor and was quietly dressing.

"You mean to go on with the investiture, I see."

She started and gave him an apprehensive look, clutching a quilted shirt to her bare breasts. "Please hear me, Godfrey. No one need ever know; Wulfric will disappear. This I take for Ranulf's sake—he died so that I might have adventure. 'Tis a small enough thing in exchange for his sacrifice." Her gaze entreated his understanding.

Godfrey's own eyes stung a bit. "Yes, that is just, a tribute for a fallen comrade."

"And the end of my boyhood." Her voice had a bitter note. "Time to put on my kirtle and, well, I know not, further than today."

"The priest will be standing ready. We could have him call the banns."

Her head jerked back, lips parted in surprise.

"I did not think to say this naked, but—" He rose from the pallet and took her hand. "Will you become my wife, the chatelaine of my manor, mother of my heirs? Please?"

Though a proven warrior, she reacted like any other woman presented with an offer of marriage. A blush swept over her face; her jaw dropped then shut with a click.

He couldn't help teasing. "Your pardon, Lady Wilfreda. By right, I should be requesting your hand of your father."

"No! I mean, *yes!* As a widow, I can speak for myself, but Sir, er, Godfrey, there's more to marriage than this." She grimaced and indicated the rumpled pallet. "A man like you should take a *lady* to wife. I've more skill with a sword than a needle."

"Wilfreda, I cannot match the Earl for riches, but I've wealth aplenty not to need a woman to be my drudge. I can suit myself in the matter of a wife. When I recall the battle just past, it is of Wulfric that I think. Standing o'er me, whirling his sword like a berserker to defend me as I lay helpless. For such a woman the life of cradle, cook pot and rosary could hardly be enough."

He took her face in both his hands, looking deep into the troubled blue-green eyes that, unbeknownst, had pierced his soul from the start. "I long to see the babes we make together—

that task is yours—but it won't be all embroidery and counting sheets. My home boasts fine hunting and hawking." He warmed to the idea as he spoke. "And my lands are spread about, for much of the year we'll be on the move, collecting rents and portions. We could even go on pilgrimage, if you like. Christendom is wide, Wilfreda, with much adventure for those who seek it. So, what say you?"

"I believe I've already accepted you." Joy transformed the boyish face to that of a woman, shining with love. The shirt dropped to the ground as their bodies met, length against length, and their mouths sought each other's.

After a long moment, Godfrey pulled back. "One thing, love."

She waited, anxious, breathless.

"Will you mind if, after all, we wait till we're home in England to wed? The thought of explaining to the priest and the Earl that I want to marry my squire brings back my headache."

About the Authors

LIZZIE ASHWORTH resides in her deep woods refuge in the western Arkansas Boston Mountains. There, she toys with words, battles with paragraphs and muses on the wind in the trees.

JACQUELINE BROCKER is an Australian writer living in the United Kingdom. Her short erotic fiction has appeared in anthologies such as *Smut Alfresco* (House of Erotica) and *Under Her Thumb* (Cleis Press). Her novella *Body & Bow* and short story "Oasis Beckoning" have been published by Forbidden Fiction.

SUSANNAH CHAPIN has been a military wife, world traveler, almost-groupie and preschool teacher. Naturally, the next logical step was writing erotic romance. She lives in Texas where she can be found reading, writing, mommying, and making a homemade chocolate pudding that will make you want to slap your mama.

LAYLA CHASE, on a dare from a close friend, challenged herself to explore the steamier side of romance and discovered all sorts of characters whose stories needed sharing. She writes contemporary and historical stories from her mountain home in California that she shares with her longtime husband and two dogs.

BEATRIX ELLROY is an ex-librarian bookhound with a love of words, the dirtier the better. She's a recent entrant into the world of erotica writing. Previous work has included everything from articles about computer games to literary fiction, but erotica is her passion and her weakness.

EMMA JAY has been writing longer than she'd care to admit, using her endless string of celebrity crushes as inspiration for her heroes. Married twenty-six years, she discovered her husband has way more tolerance for screensavers and hunk-decorated blog posts when she calls them her "heroes."

REGINA KAMMER writes erotica and historical erotic romance. She has been published by Cleis Press, Go Deeper Press, Ellora's Cave and her own imprint, Viridium Press. She began writing historical fiction during NaNoWriMo 2006, switching to erotica when all her characters suddenly demanded to have sex.

AXA LEE claims there's always someone naked in her imagination somewhere. The story begins with a glimmer, with a line, and spins from there. She spends her days with strong coffee, good beer and healthy food. She likes sweet coffee, voluptuous cows and happy men. Her writing helps feed her pastured poultry.

RENEE LUKE is a multi-published author who has written for several houses, but is now self-publishing. She writes stories with rich texture, deep emotions and realistic characters. She creates stories where sensual seduces erotic, and believes in love, romance and happily-ever-afters.

ANYA RICHARDS lives with her husband, kids, an adorable mutt and a cat that plots world domination, one food bowl at a time. The humans leave her alone when she's writing; the animals see her preoccupation as a goad.

TERRY SPEAR has written more than fifty paranormal romance novels and four medieval Highland historical romances. Her first werewolf romance, *Heart of the Wolf*, was named a 2008 *Publishers Weekly* Best Book of the Year, and her subsequent titles have garnered high praise and hit the *USA Today* best-seller list.

CONNIE WILKINS, who also writes and edits as Sacchi Green, has published stories in a hip-high stack of erotic books and edited eight anthologies, including *Lesbian Cowboys* (winner of a Lambda Literary Award) and *Wild Girls, Wild Nights* (Cleis Press). Her collection *A Ride to Remember* is published by Lethe Press.

CELA WINTER took up writing after a career as a restaurant chef (really). She has published erotic fiction in print and on the web. A resident of the Pacific Northwest, she is working on a novel—when the Muse isn't distracting her with short-story ideas.

ABOUT THE EDITOR

DELILAH DEVLIN is a *USA Today* bestselling author of erotica and erotic romance. She has published over a hundred and twenty erotic stories in multiple genres and lengths, and she is published by Atria/Strebor, Avon, Berkley, Black Lace, Cleis Press, Ellora's Cave, Harlequin Spice, HarperCollins Mischief, Kensington, Montlake Romance, Running Press and Samhain Publishing. In May 2014, she added Grand Central to her list of publishers when *Her Only Desire* was released!

Her short stories have appeared in multiple Cleis Press collections, including *Lesbian Cowboys*, *Girl Crush*, *Fairy Tale Lust*, *Lesbian Lust*, *Passion*, *Lesbian Cops*, *Dream Lover*, *Carnal Machines*, *Best Erotic Romance 2012*, *Suite Encounters*, *Girl Fever*, *Girls Who Score*, *Duty and Desire* and *Best Lesbian Romance 2013*. She has edited Cleis Press's *Girls Who Bite*, *She Shifters*, *Cowboy Lust*, *Smokin' Hot Firemen*, *High Octane Heroes* and *Cowboy Heat*.